YO-BXC-112

THE COWBOYS

They rode hard, played hard, fought hard,
and loved hard. This collection captures
the grit and daring of the red-blooded men
who lived their lives on the range.

THE BEST OF THE WEST

Anthologies of new and old stories written
with gusto and realism by your favorite
Western authors.

THE COWBOYS

Edited by Bill Pronzini & Martin H. Greenberg

FAWCETT GOLD MEDAL • NEW YORK

A Fawcett Gold Medal Book.
Published by Ballantine Books

Library of Congress Catalog Card Number: 84-91797

ISBM: 0-449-12720-6

Manufactured in the United States of America.

First Edition: May 1985

ACKNOWLEDGMENTS

"Old-Time Cowboys," S. Omar Barker. Copyright © 1968 by S. Omar Barker. From *Rawhide Rhymes*. Reprinted by permission of the author.

"Scars," Theodore Sturgeon. Copyright © 1949 by Theodore Sturgeon. First published in *Zane Grey Western Magazine*. Reprinted by permission of the author and his agents, Kirby McCauley, Ltd.

"Trail Fever," S. Omar Barker. Copyright © 1954 by The Curtis Publishing Co., Inc.; copyright © 1964 by S. Omar Barker. First published in *The Saturday Evening Post*. Reprinted by permission of the author.

"The Therefore Hog," A. B. Guthrie, Jr. Copyright © 1959 by A. B. Guthrie, Jr. From *The Big It and Other Stories*. Reprinted by permission of the author.

"Fear in the Saddle," H. S. De Rosso. Copyright © 1952 by A. B. Guthrie, Jr. from *The Big It and Other Stories*. Reprinted by permission of the author and the author's agents, Scott Meredith Literary Agency, Inc., 845 Third Avenue, New York, N.Y. 10022.

"The Nagual," Elmore Leonard. Copyright © Z-Gun Western 1956. First published in *Z-Gun Western Magazine*. Reprinted by permission of the author.

"Man on the Wagon Tongue," Elmer Kelton. Copyright © 1962 by Elmer Kelton. First published in *They Won Their Spurs*. Reprinted by permission of the author.

"Markers," Bill Pronzini. Copyright © 1982 by Western Writers of America, Inc. First published in *Roundup*. Reprinted by permission of the author.

"Isley's Stranger," Clay Fisher. Copyright © 1962 by Clay Fisher. From the 1962 Clay Fisher anthology *The Oldest Maiden Lady in Mew Mexico and Other Stories*. Library of Congress card number: 62-19423. Reprinted by permission of the author.

CONTENTS

INTRODUCTION

The Cowboys is the third in a series of *Best of the West* anthologies dedicated to making the finest in short Western fiction available to contemporary readers. In the first two books in the series, *The Lawmen* and *The Outlaws*, we brought you stories of the famous, the near-famous, and the unsung among Old West peace officers and lawbreakers; in *The Cowboys* you will find some of the finest tales ever penned over the past century about working cowboys, cattle drives, drovers, life on the range, and much, much more.

We have tried to find stories about *real* cowboys—their problems, their loneliness, and the dangers they faced—and we think we have succeeded. The life of the cowboy in the Old West was certainly not that depicted in Western films; they were black and white, dirty most of the time, and frequently broke. But, as several of these stories indicate, they fought hard and could also have a good time.

Future *Best of the West* anthologies will contain stories about the Indian, both good and bad, and the men who built and rode and, in some cases, stole from the railroads and the great steamboats—stories by such important writers in the field as Clay Fisher, Dorothy M. Johnson, Will Henry, Brian Garfield, John Jakes, and many more.

May *The Cowboys*, and all the other anthologies in the series, give you many hours of reading enjoyment.

—Bill Pronzini and
Martin H. Greenberg

The poet laureate of the Old West is unquestionably S. Omar Barker, who has published hundreds of fine and pithy verses on Western themes. The best of these, among them "Old-Time Cowboys," can be found in his 1968 collection, Rawhide Rhymes.

Old-Time Cowboys

S. Omar Barker

Proudly they rode, those horseback men
Whose like we shall not see again,
Those cowboys of a day long gone
Who saddled broncs before the dawn
To ride the long day into night—
Clan cousins of the Ishmaelite.

Their marching music was the bawl
Of longhorn cattle, and the call
Of high adventure stirred their blood
To horseback pride and hardihood.

Dusty they rode. The salt of sweat
Was more to them than the alphabet,
And more the drum of a horse's hoof
Than any fireside, field, or roof.

Partners of wind, their spurs are rust,
Their cattle trails long-settled dust,
But over their campfires' ashened embers,
The steadfast northern star remembers
That proudly they rode, with the ancient pride
Of all bold men and true who ride!

Owen Wister (1860–1938) is best known, of course, as the author of the prototype Western novel, The Virginian, first published in 1902. But he also wrote many other novels and stories of the Old West, several of which feature that classic cowboy character, Lin McLean. "The Winning of the Biscuit-Shooter" is perhaps the finest of the McLean tales—and also features the Virginian as well.

The Winning of the Biscuit-Shooter

Owen Wister

It was quite clear to me that Mr. McLean could not know the news. Meeting him to-day had been unforeseen—unforeseen and so pleasant that the thing had never come into my head until just now, after both of us had talked and dined our fill, and were torpid with satisfaction.

I had found Lin here at Riverside in the morning. At my horse's approach to the cabin, it was he and not the postmaster who had come precipitately out of the door.

"I'm turrible pleased to see yu'," he had said, immediately.

"What's happened?" said I, in some concern at his appearance.

And he piteously explained: "Why, I've been here all alone since yesterday!"

This was indeed all; and my hasty impressions of shooting and a corpse gave way to mirth over the child and his innocent grievance that he had blurted out before I could get off my horse.

Since when, I inquired of him, had his own company become such a shock to him?

"As to that," replied Mr. McLean, a thought ruffled, "when a man expects lonesomeness he stands it like he stands anything else, of course. But when he has figured on finding company—say"—he broke off (and vindictiveness sparkled in his eye)—"when you're lucky enough to catch yourself alone, why, I suppose yu' just take a chair and chat to yourself for hours—You've not seen anything of Tommy?" he pursued, with interest.

I had not; and forthwith Lin poured out to me the pent-up complaints and sociability with which he was bursting. The foreman had sent him over here with a sackful of letters for the post, and to bring back the week's mail for the ranch. A day was gone now, and nothing for a man to do but sit and sit. Tommy was overdue fifteen hours. Well, you could have endured that, but the neighbors had all locked their cabins and gone to Buffalo. It was circus week in Buffalo. Had I ever considered the money there must be in the circus business? Tommy had taken the outgoing letters early yesterday. Nobody had kept him waiting. By all rules he should have been back again last night. Maybe the stage was late reaching Powder River, and Tommy had had to lay over for it. Well, that would justify him. For more likely he had gone to the circus himself and taken the mail with him. Tommy was no type of man for postmaster. Except drawing the allowance his mother in the East gave him the first of every month, he had never shown punctuality that Lin could remember. Never had any second thoughts, and awful few first ones. Told bigger lies than a small man ought, also.

"Has successes, though," said I, wickedly.

"Huh!" went on Mr. McLean. "Successes! One ice-cream-soda success. And she"—Lin's still wounded male pride made him plaintive—"why, even that girl quit him, once she got the chance to appreciate how insignificant he was compared with the size of his words. No, sir. Not one of 'em retains interest in Tommy."

Lin was unsaddling and looking after my horse, just because he was glad to see me. Since our first acquaintance, that memorable summer of Pitchstone Canon when he had taken such good care of me and such bad care of himself, I had learned pretty well about horses and camp craft in general. He was an entire boy then. But he had been East since, East by a route of his own discovering—and from his account of that journey it had proved, I think, a sort of spiritual experience. And then the years of our friendship were beginning to roll up. Manhood of the body he had always richly possessed; and now, whenever we met after a season's absence and spoke those invariable words which all old friends upon this earth use to each other at meeting—"You haven't changed, you haven't changed at all!"—I would wonder if manhood had arrived in Lin's boy soul. And so to-day, while he attended to my horse and explained the nature of Tommy (a subject he dearly loved just now), I looked at him and took an intimate, superior pride in feeling how much more mature I was than he, after all.

There's nothing like a sense of merit for making one feel aggrieved, and on our return to the cabin Mr. McLean pointed with disgust to some firewood.

"Look at those sorrowful toothpicks," said he; "Tommy's work."

So Lin, the excellent hearted, had angrily busied himself and chopped a pile of real logs that would last a week. He had also cleaned the stove, and nailed up the bed, the pillow-end of which was on the floor. It appeared the master of the house had been sleeping in it the reverse way on account of the slant. Thus had Lin cooked and dined alone, supped alone, and sat over some old newspapers until bedtime alone with his sense of virtue. And now here it was long after breakfast, and no Tommy yet.

"It's good yu' come this forenoon," Lin said to me. "I'd not have had the heart to get up another dinner just for myself. Let's eat rich!"

Accordingly, we had richly eaten, Lin and I. He had gone out among the sheds and caught some eggs (that is how he spoke of it), we had opened a number of things in cans, and I had made my famous dish of evaporated apricots, in which I managed to fling a suspicion of caramel throughout the stew.

"Tommy'll be hot about these," said Lin, joyfully, as we ate the eggs. "He don't mind what yu' use of his canned goods—

pickled salmon and truck. He is hospitable all right enough till it comes to an egg. Then he'll tell any lie. But shucks! Yu' can read Tommy right through his clothing. 'Make yourself at home, Lin,' says he, yesterday. And he showed me his fresh milk and his stuff. 'Here's a new ham,' says he; 'too bad my damned hens ain't been layin'. The sons-o'-guns have quit on me ever since Christmas.' And away he goes to Powder River for the mail. 'You swore too heavy about them hens,' thinks I. Well, I expect he may have traveled half a mile by the time I'd found four nests.''

I am fond of eggs, and eat them constantly—and in Wyoming they were always a luxury. But I never forget those that day, and how Lin and I enjoyed them thinking of Tommy. Perhaps manhood was not quite established in my own soul at that time—and perhaps that is the reason why it is the only time I have ever known which I would live over again, those years when people said, ''You are old enough to know better''—and one didn't care!

Salmon, apricots, eggs, we dealt with them all properly, and I had some cigars. It was now that the news came back into my head.

''What do you think of—'' I began, and stopped.

I spoke out of a long silence, the slack, luxurious silence of digestion. I got no answer, naturally, from the torpid Lin, and then it occurred to me that he would have asked me what I thought, long before this, had he known. So, observing how comfortable he was, I began differently.

''What is the most important event that can happen in this country?'' said I.

Mr. McLean heard me where he lay along the floor of the cabin on his back, dozing by the fire; but his eyes remained closed. He waggled one limp, open hand slightly at me, and torpor resumed her dominion over him.

''I want to know what you consider the most important event that can happen in this country,'' said I, again, enunciating each word with slow clearness.

The throat and lips of Mr. McLean moved, and a sulky sound came forth that I recognized to be meant for the word ''War.''

Then he rolled over so that his face was away from me, and put an arm over his eyes.

"I don't mean country in the sense of United States," said I. "I mean this country here, and Bear Creek, and well, the ranches southward for fifty miles, say. Important to this section."

"Mosquitoes'll be due in about three weeks," said Lin. "Yu' might leave a man rest till then."

"I want your opinion," said I.

"Oh, misery! Well, a raise in the price of steers."

"No."

"Yu' said yu' wanted my opinion," said Lin. "Seems like yu' merely figure on givin' me yours."

"Very well," said I. "Very well, then."

I took up a copy of the Cheyenne *Sun*. It was five weeks old, and I soon perceived that I had read it three weeks ago; but I read it again for some minutes now.

"I expect a railroad would be more important," said Mr. McLean, persuasively, from the floor.

"Than a rise in steers?" said I, occupied with the Cheyenne *Sun*. "Oh, yes. Yes, a railroad certainly would."

"It's got to be money, anyhow," stated Lin, thoroughly wakened. "Money in some shape."

"How little you understand the real wants of the country!" said I, coming to the point. "It's a girl."

Mr. McLean lay quite still on the floor.

"A girl," I repeated. "A new girl coming to this starved country."

The cow-puncher took a long, gradual stretch and began to smile. "Well," said he, "yu' caught me—if that's much to do when a man is half-witted with dinner and sleep." He closed his eyes again and lay with a specious expression of indifference. But that sort of thing is a solitary entertainment, and palls. "Starved," he presently muttered. "We are kind o' starved that way, I'll admit. More dollars than girls to the square mile. And to think of all of us nice, healthy, young—bet yu' I know who she is!" he triumphantly cried. He had sat up and leveled a finger at me with the throwdown jerk of a marksman. "Sidney, Nebraska."

I nodded. This was not the lady's name—he could not recall her name—but his geography of her was accurate.

One day in February my friend, Mrs. Taylor, over on Bear Creek, had received a letter—no common event for her. Therefore, during several days she had all callers read it just as naturally as she had them all see the new baby; and baby and letter had both been brought out for me. The letter was signed,

> "Ever your afectionite frend
> "Katie Peck."

and was not easy to read, here and there. But you could piece out the drift of it, and there was Mrs. Taylor by your side, eager to help you when you stumbled. Miss Peck wrote that she was overworked in Sidney, Nebraska, and needed a holiday. When the weather grew warm she should like to come to Bear Creek and be like old times. "Like to come and be like old times" filled Mrs. Taylor with sentiment and the cow-punchers with expectation. But it is a long way from February to warm weather on Bear Creek, and even cow-punchers will forget about a new girl if she does not come. For several weeks I had not heard Miss Peck mentioned, and old girls had to do. Yesterday, however, when I paid a visit to Miss Molly Wood (the Bear Creek school-mistress), I found her keeping in order the cabin and the children of the Taylors, while they were gone forty-five miles to the stage station to meet their guest.

"Well," said Lin, judicially, "Miss Wood is a lady."

"Yes," said I, with deep gravity. For I was thinking of an occasion when Mr. McLean had discovered that truth somewhat abruptly.

Lin thoughtfully continued. "She is—she's—she's—what are you laughin' at?"

"Oh, nothing. You don't see quite so much of Miss Wood as you used to, do you?"

"Huh! So that's got around. Well, o' course I'd ought t've knowed better, I suppose. All the same, there's lots of girls do like gettin' kissed against their wishes—and you know it."

"But the point would rather seem to be that she—"

"Would rather seem! Don't yu' start that professor style o'

yours, or I'll—I'll talk more wickedness in worse language than ever yu've heard me do yet."

"Impossible!" I murmured, sweetly, and Master Lin went on.

"As to point—that don't need to be explained to me. She's a lady all right." He ruminated for a moment. "She has about scared all the boys off, though," he continued. "And that's what you get by being refined," he concluded, as if Providence had at length spoken in this matter.

"She has not scared off a boy from Virginia, I notice," said I. "He was there yesterday afternoon again. Ridden all the way over from Sunk Creek. Didn't seem particularly frightened."

"Oh, well, nothin' alarms him—not even refinement," said Mr. McLean, with his grin. "And she'll fool your Virginian like she done the balance of us. You wait. Shucks! If all the girls were that chilly, why, what would us poor punchers do?"

"You have me cornered," said I, and we sat in a philosophical silence, Lin on the floor still, and I at the window. There I looked out upon a scene my eyes never tired of then, nor can my memory now. Spring had passed over it with its first, lightest steps. The pastured levels undulated in emerald. Through the many-changing sage, that just this moment of to-day was lilac, shone greens scarce a week old in the dimples of the foot-hills; and greens new-born beneath to-day's sun melted among them. Around the doublings of the creek in the willow thickets glimmered skeined veils of yellow and delicate crimson. The stream poured turbulently away from the snows of the mountains behind us. It went winding in many folds across the meadows into distance and smallness, and so vanished round the great red battlement of wall beyond. Upon this were falling the deep hues of afternoon—violet, rose, and saffron, swimming and meeting as if some prism had dissolved and flowed over the turrets and crevices of the sandstone. Far over there I saw a dot move.

"At last!" said I.

Lin looked out of the window. "It's more than Tommy," said he, at once; and his eyes made it out before mine could. "It's a wagon. That's Tommy's bald-faced horse alongside.

He's fooling to the finish," Lin severely commented, as if, after all this delay, there should at least be a homestretch.

Presently, however, a homestretch seemed likely to occur. The bald-faced horse executed some lively maneuvers, and Tommy's voice reached us faintly through the light spring air. He was evidently howling the remarkable strain of yells that the cow-punchers invented as the speech best understood by cows —"Oi-ee, yah, whoop-yahoye-ee, oooo-oop, oop, oop-oop-oop-oop-yah-hee!" But that gives you no idea of it. Alphabets are worse than photographs. It is not the lungs of every man that can produce these effects, nor even from armies, eagles, or mules were such sounds ever heard on earth. The cow-puncher invented them. And when the last cow-puncher is laid to rest (if that, alas, has not already befallen) the yells will be forever gone. Singularly enough, the cattle appeared to appreciate them. Tommy always did them very badly, and that was plain even at this distance. Nor did he give us a homestretch, after all. The bald-faced horse made a number of revolutions and returned beside the wagon.

"Showin' off," remarked Lin. "Tommy's showin' off." Suspicion crossed his face, and then certainty. "Why, we might have knowed that!" he exclaimed, in a dudgeon. "It's her." He hastened outside for a better look, and I came to the door myself. "That's what it is," said he. "It's the girl. Oh, yes. That's Taylor's buckskins—they're four-year-olds. Or else—anyway, they laid over last night at Powder River, and Tommy he has just laid over too, yu' see, holdin' the mail back on us twenty-four hours—and that's your postmaster!"

It was our postmaster, and this he had done, quite as the virtuously indignant McLean surmised. Had I taken the same interest in the new girl, I suppose that I, too, should have felt virtuously indignant.

Lin and I stood outside to receive the travelers. As their cavalcade drew near, Mr. McLean grew silent and watchful, his whole attention focused upon the Taylors' vehicle. Its approach was joyous. Its gear made a cheerful clanking. Taylor cracked his whip, and encouragingly chirruped to his buckskins, and Tommy's apparatus jingled musically. For Tommy wore upon himself and his saddle all the things you can wear in the Wild

West. Except that his hair was not long, our postmaster might have conducted a show and minted gold by exhibiting his romantic person before the eyes of princes. He began with a black-and-yellow rattlesnake skin for a hat-band, he continued with a fringed and beaded shirt of buckskin, and concluded with large, tinkling spurs. Of course, there were things between his shirt and his heels, but all leather and deadly weapons. He had also a riata, a cuerta, and tapaderos, and frequently employed these Spanish names for the objects. I wish that I had not lost Tommy's photograph in Rocky Mountain costume. You must understand that he was really pretty, with blue eyes, ruddy cheeks, and a graceful figure; and besides, he had twenty-four hours' start of poor dusty Lin, whose best clothes were elsewhere.

You might have supposed that it would be Mrs. Taylor who should present us to her friend from Sidney, Nebraska; but Tommy on his horse undertook the office before the wagon had well come to a standstill. "Good friends of mine, and gentlemen, both," said he to Miss Peck; and to us, "A lady whose acquaintance will prove a treat to our section."

We all bowed at each other beneath the florid expanse of these recommendations, and I was proceeding to murmur something about its being a long journey and a fine day when Miss Peck cut me short, gayly:

"Well," she exclaimed to Tommy, "I guess I'm pretty near ready for them eggs you've spoke so much about."

I had not often seen Mr. McLean lose his presence of mind. He needed merely to exclaim, "Why, Tommy, you told me your hens had not been laying since Christmas!" and we could have sat quiet and let Tommy try to find all the eggs that he could. But the new girl was a sore embarrassment to the cowpuncher's wits. Poor Lin stood by the wheels of the wagon. He looked up at Miss Peck, he looked over at Tommy, his features assumed a rueful expression, and he wretchedly blurted:

"Why, Tommy, I've been and eat 'em!"

"Well, if that ain't!" cried Miss Peck. She stared with interest at Lin as he now assisted her to descend.

"All?" faltered Tommy. "Not the four nests?"

"I've had three meals, yu' know," Lin reminded him, deprecatingly.

"I helped him," said I. "Ten innocent, fresh eggs. But we have left some ham. Forgive us, please."

"I declare!" said Miss Peck, abruptly, and rolled her sluggish, inviting eyes upon me. "You're a case, too, I expect."

But she took only brief note of me, although it was from head to foot. In her stare the dull shine of familiarity grew vacant, and she turned back to Lin McLean. "You carry that," said she, and gave the pleased cow-puncher a hand valise.

"I'll look after your things, Miss Peck!" called Tommy, now springing down from his horse. The egg tragedy had momentarily stunned him.

"You'll attend to the mail first, Mr. Postmaster!" said the lady, but favoring him with a look from her large eyes. "There's plenty of gentlemen here." With that her glance favored Lin. She went into the cabin, he following her close, with the Taylors and myself in the rear. "Well, I guess I'm about collapsed!" said she, vigorously, and sank upon one of Tommy's chairs.

The fragile article fell into sticks beneath her, and Lin leaped to her assistance. He placed her upon a firmer foundation. Mrs. Taylor brought a basin and towel to bathe the dust from her face, Mr. Taylor produced whiskey, and I found sugar and hot water. Tommy would doubtless have done something in the way of assistance or restoratives, but he was gone to the stable with the horses.

"Shall I get your medicine from the valise, deary?" inquired Mrs. Taylor.

"Not now," her visitor answered; and I wondered why she should take such a quick look at me.

"We'll soon have yu' independent of medicine," said Lin, gallantly. "Our climate and scenery here has frequently raised the dead."

"You're a case, anyway!" exclaimed the sick lady, with rich conviction.

The cow-puncher now sat himself on the edge of Tommy's bed, and, throwing one leg across the other, began to raise her spirits with cheerful talks. She steadily watched him—his face sometimes, sometimes his lounging, masculine figure. While he thus devoted his attentions to her, Taylor departed to help Tommy at the stable, and good Mrs. Taylor, busy with supper for all of us in the kitchen, expressed her joy at having her old friend of childhood for a visit after so many years.

"Sickness has changed poor Katie some," said she. "But I'm hoping she'll get back her looks on Bear Creek."

"She seems less feeble than I had understood," I remarked.

"Yes, indeed! I do believe she's feeling stronger. She was that tired and down yesterday with the long stage ride, and it is so lonesome! But Taylor and I heartened her up, and Tommy came with the mail, and to-day she's real spruced-up like, feeling she's among friends."

"How long will she stay?" I inquired.

"Just as long as ever she wants! Me and Katie hasn't met since we was young girls in Dubuque, for I left home when I married Taylor, and he brought me to this country right soon; and it ain't been like Dubuque much, though if I had it to do over again I'd do just the same, as Taylor knows. Katie and me hasn't wrote even, not till this February, for you always mean to and you don't. Well, it'll be like old times. Katie'll be most thirty-four, I expect. Yes. I was seventeen and she was sixteen the very month I was married. Poor thing! She ought to have got some good man for a husband, but I expect she didn't have any chance, for there was a big fam'ly o' them girls, and old Peck used to act real scandalous, getting drunk so folks didn't visit there evenings scarcely at all. And so she quit home, it seems, and got a position in the railroad eating-house at Sidney, and now she has poor health with feeding them big trains day and night."

"A biscuit-shooter!" said I.

Loyal Mrs. Taylor stirred some batter in silence. "Well," said she then, "I'm told that's what the yard-hands of the railroad called them poor waiter-girls. You might hear it around the switches at them division stations."

I had heard it in higher places also, but meekly accepted the reproof.

If you have made your trans-Missouri journeys only since the new era of dining-cars, there is a quantity of things you have come too late for, and will never know. Three times a day in the brave days of old you sprang from your scarce-halted car at the summons of a gong. You discerned by instinct the right direction, and, passing steadily through doorways, had taken, before you knew it, one of some sixty chairs in a room of tables and catsup bottles. Behind the chairs, standing attention, a platoon of Amazons, thick-wristed, pink-and-blue, began immediately a swift chant. It hymned the total bill-of-fare at a blow. In this inexpressible ceremony the name of every dish went hurtling into the next, telescoped to shapelessness. Moreover, if you stopped your Amazon in the middle, it dislocated her, and she merely went back and took a fresh start. The chant was always the same, but you never learned it. As soon as it began, your mind snapped shut like the upper berth in a Pullman. You must have uttered appropriate words—even a parrot will—for next you were eating things—pie, ham, hot cakes—as fast as you could. Twenty minutes of swallowing, and all aboard for Ogden, with your pile-driven stomach dumb with amazement. The Strasbourg goose is not dieted with greater velocity, and "biscuit-shooter" is a grand word. Very likely some Homer of the railroad yards first said it—for what men upon the present earth so speak with imagination's tongue as we Americans?

If Miss Peck had been a biscuit-shooter, I could account readily for her conversation, her equipped deportment, the maturity in her round, blue, marble eye. Her abrupt laugh, something beyond gay, was now sounding in response to Mr. McLean's lively sallies, and I found him fanning her into convalescence with his hat. She herself made but few remarks, but allowed the cow-puncher to entertain her, merely exclaiming briefly now and then "I declare!" and "If you ain't!" Lin was most certainly engaging, if that was the lady's meaning. His wide-open eyes sparkled upon her, and he half closed them now and then to look at her more effectively. I suppose she was worth it to him. I have forgotten to say that she was handsome in a large California-fruit style. They made a good-looking pair of animals. But it was in the presence of Tommy that Master Lin shone more energetically than ever, and under such shining Tommy was transparently restless. He tried, and failed, to bring the conversation his way, and took to rearranging the mail and the furniture.

"Supper's ready," he said, at length. "Come right in, Miss Peck; right in here. This is your seat—this one, please. Now you can see my fields out of the window."

"You sit here," said the biscuit-shooter to Lin; and thus she was between them. "Them's elegant!" she presently exclaimed to Tommy. "Did you cook 'em?"

I explained that the apricots were of my preparation.

"Indeed!" said she, and returned to Tommy, who had been telling her of his ranch, his potatoes, his horses. "And do you punch cattle, too?" she inquired of him.

"Me?" said Tommy, slightingly; "gave it up years ago; too empty a life for me. I leave that to such as like it. When a man owns his own property"—Tommy swept his hand at the whole landscape—"he takes to more intellectual work."

"Lickin' postage-stamps," Mr. McLean suggested, sourly.

"You lick them and I cancel them," answered the postmaster; and it does not seem a powerful rejoinder. But Miss Peck uttered her laugh.

"That's one on you," she told Lin. And throughout this meal it was Tommy who had her favor. She partook of his generous supplies; she listened to his romantic inventions, the trails he had discovered, the bears he had slain; and after supper it was with Tommy, and not with Lin, that she went for a little walk.

"Katie was ever a tease," said Mrs. Taylor, of her childhood friend, and Mr. Taylor observed that there was always safety in numbers. "She'll get used to the ways of this country quicker than our little school-marm," said he.

Mr. McLean said very little, but read the newly arrived papers. It was only when bedtime dispersed us, the ladies in the cabin and the men choosing various spots outside, that he became talkative again for a while. We lay in the blankets we had spread on some soft, dry sand in preference to the stable, where Taylor and Tommy had gone. Under the contemplative influence of the stars, Lin fell into generalization.

"Ever notice," said he, "how whiskey and lyin' act the same on a man?"

I did not feel sure that I had.

"Just the same way. You keep either of 'em up long enough, and yu' get to require it. If Tommy didn't lie some every day, he'd get sick."

I was sleepy, but I murmured assent to this, and trusted he would not go on.

"Ever notice," said he, "how the victims of the whiskey and lyin' habit get to increasing the dose?"

"Yes," said I.

"Him roping six bears!" pursued Mr. McLean, after further contemplation. "Or any bear. Ever notice how the worser a man's lyin' the silenter other men'll get? Why's that, now?"

I believe that I made a faint sound to imply that I was following him.

"Men don't get took in. But ladies now, they—"

Here he paused again, and during the next interval of contemplation I sank beyond his reach.

In the morning I left Riverside for Buffalo, and there or thereabouts I remained for a number of weeks. Miss Peck did not enter my thoughts, nor did I meet anyone to remind me of her, until one day I stopped at the drugstore. It was not for drugs, but gossip, that I went. In the daytime there was no place like the apothecary's for meeting men and hearing the news. There I heard how things were going everywhere, including Bear Creek.

All the cow-punchers liked the new girl up there, said gossip. She was a great addition to society. Reported to be more companionable than the school-marm, Miss Molly Wood, who had been raised too far east, and showed it. Vermont, or some such dude place. Several had been in town buying presents for Miss Katie Peck. Tommy Postmaster had paid high for a necklace of elktushes the government scout at McKinney sold him. Too bad Miss Peck did not enjoy good health. Shorty had been in only yesterday to get her medicine again. Third bottle. Had I heard the big joke on Lin McLean? He had promised her the skin of a big bear he knew the location of, and Tommy got the bear.

Two days after this I joined one of the round-up camps at sunset. They had been working from Salt Creek to Bear Creek, and the Taylor ranch was in visiting distance from them again, after an interval of gathering and branding far across the country. The Virginian, the gentle-voiced Southerner, whom I had last seen lingering with Miss Wood, was in camp. Silent three-quarters of the time, as was his way, he sat gravely watching Lin McLean. That person seemed silent also, as was not his way quite so much.

"Lin," said the Southerner, "I reckon you're failin'."

Mr. McLean raised a somber eye, but did not trouble to answer further.

"A healthy man's laigs ought to fill his pants," pursued the Virginian.

The challenged puncher stretched out a limb and showed his muscles with young pride.

"And yu' cert'nly take no comfort in your food," his ingenious friend continued, slowly and gently.

"I'll eat you a match any day and place yu' name," said Lin.

"It ain't sca'cely hon'able," went on the Virginian, "to waste away durin' the round-up. A man owes his strength to them that hires it. If he is paid to rope stock he ought to rope stock, and not leave it didge or pull away."

"It's not many didge my rope," boasted Lin imprudently.

"Why, they tell me as how that heifer of the Sidney-Nebraska brand got plumb away from yu' and little Tommy had to chase afteh her."

Lin sat up angrily amid the laughter, but reclined again. "I'll improve," said he, "if yu' learn me how yu' rope that Vermont stock so handy. Has she promised to be your sister yet?" he added.

"Is that what they do?" inquired the Virginian, serenely. "I have never got related that way. Why, that'll make Tommy your brother-in-law, Lin!"

And now, indeed, the camp laughed a loud, merciless laugh.

But Lin was silent. Where everybody lives in a glass-house the victory is to him who throws the adroitest stone. Mr. McLean was readier witted than most, but the gentle, slow Virginian could be a master when he chose.

"Tommy has been recountin' his wars up at the Taylors'," he now told the camp. "He has frequently campaigned with

General Crook, General Miles, and General Ruger, all at onced. He's an exciting fighter, in conversation, and kep' us all scared for mighty nigh an hour. Miss Peck appeared interested in his statements.''

"What was you doing at the Taylors' yourself?" demanded Lin.

"Vistin' Miss Wood," answered the Virginian with entire ease. For he also knew when to employ the plain truth as a bluff. "You'd ought to write to Tommy's mother, Lin, and tell her what a daredevil her son is gettin' to be. She would cut off his allowance and bring him home, and you would have the runnin' all to yourself.''

"I'll fix him yet," muttered Mr. McLean. "Him and his wars.''

With that he rose and left us.

The next afternoon he informed me that if I was riding up the creek to spend the night he would go for company. In that direction we started, therefore, without any mention of the Taylors or Miss Peck. I was puzzled. Never had I seen him thus disconcerted by woman. With him woman had been a transient disturbance. I had witnessed a series of flighty romances, where the cow-puncher had come, seen, often conquered, and moved on. Nor had his affairs been of the sort to teach a young man respect. I am putting it rather mildly.

For the first part of our way this afternoon he was moody, and after that began to speak with appalling wisdom about life. Life, he said, was a serious matter. Did I realize that? A man was liable to forget it. A man was liable to go sporting and helling around till he waked up some day and found all his best pleasures had become just a business. No interest, no surprise, no novelty left, and no cash in the bank. Shorty owed him fifty dollars. Shorty would be able to pay that after the round-up, and he, Lin, would get his time and rustle altogether some five hundred dollars. Then there was his homestead claim on Box Elder, and the surveyors were coming in this fall. No better location for a home in this country than Box Elder. Wood, water, fine land. All it needed was a house and ditches and buildings and fences, and to be planted with crops. Such chances and considerations should sober a man and make him careful what he did. "I'd take in Cheyenne on our wedding-trip, and after that I'd settle right down to improving Box Elder," concluded Mr. McLean, suddenly.

His real intentions flashed upon me for the first time. I had not remotely imagined such a step.

"*Marry* her!" I screeched in dismay. "Marry *her!*"

I don't know which word was the worse to emphasize at such a moment, but I emphasized both, thoroughly.

"I didn't expect yu'd act that way," said the lover. He dropped behind me fifty yards and spoke no more.

Not at once did I beg his pardon for the brutality I had been surprised into. It is one of those speeches that, once said, is said forever. But it was not that which withheld me. As I thought of the tone in which my friend had replied, it seemed to me sullen, rather than deeply angry or wounded—resentment at my opinion not of her character so much as of his choice! Then I began to be sorry for the fool, and schemed for a while how to intervene. But have you ever tried to intervene? I soon abandoned the idea, and took a way to be forgiven, and to learn more.

"Lin," I began, slowing my horse, "you must not think about what I said."

"I'm thinkin' of pleasanter subjects," said he, and slowed his own horse.

"Oh, look here!" I exclaimed.

"Well?" said he. He allowed his horse to come within about ten yards.

"Astonishment makes a man say anything," I proceeded. "And I'll say again you're too good for her—and I'll say I don't generally believe in the wife being older than the husband."

"What's two years?" said Lin.

I was near screeching out again, but saved myself. He was not quite twenty-five, and I remembered Mrs. Taylor's unprejudiced computation of the biscuit-shooter's years. It is a lady's prerogative, however, to estimate her own age.

"She had her twenty-seventh birthday last month," said Lin, with sentiment, bringing his horse entirely abreast of mine. "I promised her a bear-skin."

"Yes," said I, "I heard about that in Buffalo."

Lin's face grew dusky with anger. "No doubt yu' heard

about it!'' said he. "I don't guess yu' heard much about anything else. I ain't told the truth to any of 'em—but her.'' He
looked at me with a certain hesitation. "I think I will,'' he continued. "I don't mind tellin' you.''

He began to speak in a strictly business tone, while he evened
the coils of rope that hung on his saddle.

"She had spoke to me about her birthday, and I had spoke to
her about something to give her. I had offered to buy her in
town whatever she named, and I was figuring to borrow from
Taylor. But she fancied the notion of a bear-skin. I had mentioned about some cubs. I had found the cubs where the she-
bear had them cached by the foot of a big boulder in the range
over Ten Sleep, and I put back the leaves and stuff on top o'
them little things as near as I could the way I found them, so
that the bear would not suspicion me. For I was aiming to get
her. And Miss Peck, she sure wanted the hide for her birthday.
So I went back. The she-bear was off, and I clumb up inside the
rock, and I waited a turrible long spell till the sun traveled
clean around the cañon. Mrs. Bear came home, though, a big
cinnamon; and I raised my gun, but laid it down to see what
she'd do. She scrapes around and snuffs, and the cubs start
whining, and she talks back to 'em. Next she sits up awful big,
and lifts up a cub and holds it to her close with both her paws,
same as a person. And she rubbed her ear agin the cub, and the
cub sort o' nipped her, and she cuffed the cub, and the other cub
came toddlin', and away they starts rolling, all three of 'em! I
watched that for a long while. That big thing just nursed and
played with them little cubs, beatin' 'em for a change once in a
while, and talkin', and onced in a while she'd sit up solemn and
look all around so life-like that I near busted. Why, how was I
goin' to spoil that? So I come away, very quiet, you bet! for I'd
have hated to have Mrs. Bear notice me. Miss Peck, she
laughed. She claimed I was scared to shoot.''

"After you had told her why it was?'' said I.

"Before and after. I didn't tell her first, because I felt kind of
foolish. Then Tommy went and he killed the bear all right, and
she has the skin now. Of course the boys joshed me a heap
about gettin' beat by Tommy.''

"But since she has taken you?'' said I.

"She ain't said it. But she will when she understands Tommy."

I fancied that the lady understood. The once I had seen her she appeared to me as what might be termed an expert in men, and one to understand also the reality of Tommy's ranch and allowance, and how greatly these differed from Box Elder. Probably the one thing she could not understand was why Lin spared the mother and her cubs. A deserted home in Dubuque, a career in a railroad eating-house, a somewhat vague past, and a present lacking context—indeed, I hoped with all my heart that Tommy would win!

"Lin," said I, "I'm backing him."

"Back away!" said he. "Tommy can please a woman—him and his blue eyes—but he don't savvy how to make a woman want him, not any better than he knows about killin' Injuns."

"Did you hear about the Crows?" said I.

"About young bucks going on the war-path? Shucks! That's put up by the papers of this section. They're aimin' to get Uncle Sam to order his troops out, and then folks can sell hay and stuff to 'em. If Tommy believed any Crows—" He stopped, and suddenly slapped his leg.

"What's the matter now?" I asked.

"Oh, nothing." He took to singing, and his face grew roguish to its full extent. "What made yu' say that to me?" he asked, presently.

"Say what?"

"About marrying. Yu' don't think I'd better."

"I don't."

"Onced in a while yu' tell me I'm flighty. Well, I am. Whoop-ya!"

"Colts ought not to marry," said I.

"Sure!" said he. And it was not until we came in sight of the Virginian's black horse tied in front of Miss Wood's cabin next to the Taylors' that Lin changed the lively course of thought that was evidently filling his mind.

"Tell yu'," said he, touching my arm confidentially and pointing to the black horse, "for all her Vermont refinement she's a woman just the same. She likes him dangling round her so earnest—him that nobody ever saw dangle before. And he has quit spreein' with the boys. And what does he get by it? I am glad I was not raised good enough to appreciate the Miss Woods of this world,'' he added, defiantly, ''except at long range.''

At the Taylors' cabin we found Miss Wood sitting with her admirer, and Tommy from Riverside to admire Miss Peck. The biscuit-shooter might pass for twenty-seven, certainly. Something had agreed with her—whether the medicine, or the mountain air, or so much masculine company; whatever had done it, she had bloomed into brutal comeliness. Her hair looked curlier, her figure shapelier, her teeth shone whiter, and her cheeks were a lusty, overbearing red. And there sat Molly Wood talking sweetly to her big, grave Virginian; to look at them, there was no doubt that he had been ''raised good enough'' to appreciate her, no matter what had been his raising!

Lin greeted everyone jauntily. ''How are yu', Miss Peck? How are yu', Tommy?'' said he. ''Hear the news, Tommy? Crow Injuns on the war-path.''

''I declare!'' said the biscuit-shooter.

The Virginian was about to say something, but his eye met Lin's, and then he looked at Tommy. Then what he did say was, ''I hadn't been goin' to mention it to the ladies until it was right sure.''

''You needn't to be afraid, Miss Peck,'' said Tommy. ''There's lots of men here.''

''Who's afraid?'' said the biscuit-shooter.

''Oh,'' said Lin, ''maybe it's like most news we get in this country. Two weeks stale and a lie when it was fresh.''

''Of course,'' said Tommy.

''Hello, Tommy!'' called Taylor from the lane. ''Your horse has broke his rein and run down the field.''

Tommy rose in disgust and sped after the animal.

''I must be cooking supper now,'' said Katie shortly.

''I'll stir for yu','' said Lin, grinning at her.

''Come along then,'' said she; and they departed to the adjacent kitchen.

Miss Wood's gray eyes brightened with mischief. She looked at her Virginian, and she looked at me.

"Do you know," she said, "I used to be afraid that when Bear Creek wasn't new anymore it might become dull!"

"Miss Peck doesn't find it dull, either," said I.

Molly Wood immediately assumed a look of doubt. "But mightn't it become just—just a little trying to have two gentlemen so very—determined, you know?"

"Only one is determined," said the Virginian.

Molly looked inquiring.

"Lin is determined Tommy shall not beat him. That's all it amounts to."

"Dear me, what a notion!"

"No, ma'am, no notion. Tommy—well, Tommy is considered harmless, ma'am. A cow-puncher of reputation in this country would cert'nly never let Tommy get ahaid of him that way."

"It's pleasant to know sometimes how much we count!" exclaimed Molly.

"Why, ma'am," said the Virginian, surprised at her flash of indignation, "where is any countin' without some love?"

"Do you mean to say that Mr. McLean does not care for Miss Peck?"

"I reckon he thinks he does. But there is a mighty wide difference between thinkin' and feelin', ma'am."

I saw Molly's eyes drop from his, and I saw the rose deepen in her cheeks. But just then a loud voice came from the kitchen.

"You, Lin, if you try any of your foolin' with me, I'll histe yu's over the jiste!"

"All cow-punchers—" I attempted to resume.

"Quit now, Lin McLean," shouted the voice, "or I'll put yu's through that window, and it shut."

"Well, Miss Peck, I'm gettin' most a full dose o' this treatment. Ever since yu' come I've been doing my best. And yu' just cough in my face. And now I'm going to quit and cough back."

"Would you enjoy walkin' out till supper, ma'am?" inquired the Virginian as Molly rose. "You was speaking of gathering some flowers yondeh."

"Why, yes," said Molly, blithely. "And you'll come?" she added to me.

But I was on the Virginian's side. "I must look after my horse," said I, and went down to the corral.

Day was slowly going as I took my pony to the water. Corncliff Mesa, Crowheart Butte, these shone in the rays that came through the cañon. The cañon's sides lifted like tawny castles in the same light. Where I walked the odor of thousands of wild roses hung over the margin where the thickets grew. High in the upper air, magpies were sailing across the silent blue. Somewhere I could hear Tommy explaining loudly how he and General Crook had pumped lead into hundreds of Indians; and when supper-time brought us all back to the door he was finishing the account to Mrs. Taylor. Molly and the Virginian arrived bearing flowers, and he was saying that few cowpunchers had any reason for saving their money.

"But when you get old?" said she.

"We mostly don't live long enough to get old, ma'am," said he, simply. "But I have a reason, and I am saving."

"Give me the flowers," said Molly. And she left him to arrange them on the table as Lin came hurrying out.

"I've told her," said he to the Southerner and me, "that I've asked her twiced, and I'm going to let her have one more chance. And I've told her that if it's a log cabin she's marryin', why Tommy is a sure good wooden piece of furniture to put inside it. And I guess she knows there's not much wooden furniture about me. I want to speak to you." He took the Virginian round the corner. But though he would not confide in me, I began to discern something quite definite at supper.

"Cattle men will lose stock if the Crows get down as far as this," he said, casually, and Mrs. Taylor suppressed a titter.

"Ain't it hawses they're repawted as running off?" said the Virginian.

"Chap come into the round-up this afternoon," said Lin. "But he was rattled, and told a heap o' facts that wouldn't square."

"Of course they wouldn't," said Tommy, haughtily.

"Oh, there's nothing in it," said Lin, dismissing the subject.

"Have yu' been to the opera since we went to Cheyenne, Mrs. Taylor?"

Mrs. Taylor had not.

"Lin," said the Virginian, "did yu' ever see that opera 'Cyarmen'?"

"You bet. Fellow's girl quits him for a bull-fighter. Gets him up in the mountains, and quits him. He wasn't much good—not in her class o' sports, smugglin' and such."

"I reckon she was doubtful of him from the start. Took him to the mount'ins to experiment, where they'd not have interruption," said the Virginian.

"Talking of mountains," said Tommy, "this range here used to be a great place for Indians til we ran 'em out with Terry. Pumped lead into the red sons-o'-guns."

"You bet," said Lin. "Do yu' figure that girl tired of her bull-fighter and quit him, too?"

"I reckon," replied the Virginian, "that the bull-fighter wore better."

"Fans and taverns and gypsies and sportin'," said Lin. "My! but I'd like to see them countries with oranges and bull-fights! Only I expect Spain, maybe, ain't keepin' it up so gay as when 'Carmen' happened."

The table-talk soon left romance and turned upon steers and alfalfa, a grass but lately introduced in the country. No further mention was made of the hostile Crows, and from this I drew the false conclusion that Tommy had not come up to their hopes in the matter of reciting his campaigns. But when the hour came for those visitors who were not spending the night to take their leave, Taylor drew Tommy aside with me, and I noticed the Virginian speaking with Molly Wood, whose face showed diversion.

"Don't seem to make anything of it," whispered Taylor to Tommy, "but the ladies have got their minds on this Indian truck."

"Why, I'll just explain—" began Tommy.

"Don't," whispered Lin, joining us. "Yu' know how women are. Once they take a notion, why, the more yu' deny the surer they get. Now yu' see, him and me" (he jerked his elbow toward the Virginian) "must go back to camp, for we're on second relief."

"And the ladies would sleep better knowing there was another man in the house," said Taylor.

"In that case," said Tommy, "I—"

"Yu' see," said Lin, "they've been told about Ten Sleep being burned two nights ago."

"It ain't!" cried Tommy.

"Why, of course it ain't," drawled the ingenious Lin. "But that's what I say. You and I know Ten Sleep's all right, but we can't report from our own knowledge seeing it all right, and there it is. They get these nervous notions."

"Just don't appear to make anything special of not going back to Riverside," repeated Taylor, "but—"

"But just kind of stay here," said Lin.

"I will!" exclaimed Tommy. "Of course, I'm glad to oblige."

I suppose I was slow-sighted. All this pain seemed to me larger than its results. They had imposed upon Tommy, yes. But what of that? He was to be kept from going back to Riverside until morning. Unless they proposed to visit his empty cabin and play tricks—but that would be too childish, even for Lin McLean, to say nothing of the Virginian, his occasional partner in mischief.

"In spite of the Crows," I satirically told the ladies, "I shall sleep outside, as I intended. I've no use for houses at this season."

The cinches of the horses were tightened, Lin and the Virginian laid a hand on their saddle-horns, swung up, and soon all sound of the galloping horses had ceased. Molly Wood declined to be nervous, and crossed to her little neighbor cabin; we all parted, and (as always in that blessed country) deep sleep quickly came to me.

I don't know how long after it was that I sprang from my blankets in half-doubting fright. But I had dreamed nothing. A second long, wild yell now gave me (I must own to it) a horrible chill. I had no pistol—nothing. In the hateful brightness of the moon my single thought was "House! House!" and I fled across the lane in my underclothes to the cabin, when round the corner whirled the two cow-punchers, and I understood. I saw the Virginian catch sight of me in my shirt, and saw his teeth as he smiled. I hastened to my blankets, and returned more decent to stand and watch the two go shooting and yelling round the cabin, crazy with their youth. The door was opened, and Taylor courageously emerged, bearing a Winchester. He fired at the sky immediately.

"B'gosh!" he roared. "That's one." He fired again. "Out and at'em. They're running."

At this, duly came Mrs. Taylor in white with a pistol, and Miss Peck in white, staring and stolid. But no Tommy. Noise prevailed without, shots by the stable and shots by the creek. The two cow-punchers dismounted and joined Taylor. Maniac delight seized me, and I, too, rushed about with them, helping the din.

"Oh, Mr. Taylor!" said a voice. "I didn't think it of you." It was Molly Wood, come from her cabin, very pretty in a hood-and-cloak arrangement. She stood by the fence, laughing, but more at us than with us.

"Stop, friends!" said Taylor, gasping. "She teaches my Bobbie his ABC. I'd hate to have Bobbie—"

"Speak to your papa," said Molly, and held her scholar up on the fence.

"Well, I'll be gol-darned," said Taylor, surveying his costume, "if Lin McLean hasn't made a fool of me tonight!"

"Where has Tommy got?" said Mrs. Taylor.

"Didn't yu' see him?" said the biscuit-shooter, speaking her first word in all this.

We followed her into the kitchen. The table was covered with tin plates. Beneath it, wedged, knelt Tommy with a pistol firm in his hand; but the plates were rattling up and down like castanets.

There was a silence among us, and I wondered what we were going to do.

"Well," murmured the Virginian to himself, "if I could have foresaw, I'd not—it makes yu' feel humiliated yu'self."

He marched out, got on his horse, and rode away. Lin followed him, but perhaps less penitently. We all dispersed without saying anything, and presently from my blankets I saw poor Tommy come out of the silent cabin, mount, and slowly, very slowly, ride away. He would spend the night at Riverside, after all.

Of course we recovered from our unexpected shame, and the

tale of the table and the dancing plates was not told as a sad one.
But it is a sad one when you think of it.

I was not there to see Lin get his bride. I learned from the
Virginian how the victorious puncher had ridden away across
the sunny sagebrush, bearing the biscuit-shooter with him to
the nearest justice of the peace. She was astride the horse he had
brought for her.

"Yes, he beat Tommy," said the Virginian. "Some folks,
anyway, get what they want in this hyeh world."

From which I inferred that Miss Molly Wood was harder to
beat than Tommy.

*Although he is most often remembered today for his novels
and stories of the Alaska Gold Rush (The Spoilers, "The
Weight of Obligation"), and for such bestselling romances
from the period 1910–1925 as The Barrier and The Ne'er
Do Well, Rex Beach also authored a number of excellent
Western stories. Some of the best of these can be found in his
first collection, Pardners (1905)—among them this light-
hearted tale of cowboys, Indians, and a spirited game of
horse thievery.*

The Colonel and the
Horse Thief

Rex Beach

Those marks on my arm? Oh! I got 'em playin' horse thief.
Yes, playin'. I wasn't a real one, you know. Well, I s'pose it
was sort of a queer game. Came near bein' my last too.

That was way back in the sixties, when I was as wild a lad as
ever straddled a pony.

You see, five of us had gone over into the Crow Nation to
race horses with the Indians, and it was on the way back that the
horse thief business came up.

The plan had just enough risk and devilment in it to suit a
harum-scarum young feller like me; so we got five of the boys
who had good horses, lumped together all of our money, and
rode out to invade the reservation.

There was Jim Barrett, Kink Martin, a little fellow named
Hollis, Pat Donnelley, and me. I was about the best rider, and

had Martin's mare, Black Hawk, for the racing. Hollis was to ride his own horse.

You know how an Indian loves to run horses? Well, the Crows had a good deal of money then, and our scheme was to go over there, get up a big race, back our horses with all we had, and take down the wealth.

You see, as soon as the money was up and the horses started, every Indian would be watchin' the race and yellin' at the nags, then, in the confusion, our boys was to grab the whole pot, Indians' money and ours too, and we'd make our get away across the river back into Texas.

Well, sir! I never see anything work out like that scheme did. Them Crows was dead anxious to run their ponies and seemed skeered that we wouldn't let 'em get all their money up.

Donnelley was to stay in the saddle and keep the other horses close to Barrett and Martin. They was to stick next to the money, and one of 'em do the bearin' off of the booty while the other made the protection play.

We rode out from camp the next mornin' to where we'd staked out a mile track on the prairie. The Crows entered two pretty good-lookin' horses and had their jockeys stripped down to breech-clouts, while Hollis and me wore our whole outfits on our backs, as we didn't exactly figger on dressin' after the race, leastways, not on that side of the river.

Just before we lined up, Jim says: "Now you-all ride like hell, and when you git to the far turn we'll let the guns loose and stampede the crowd. Then just leave the track and make a break for the river, everybody for himself. We'll all meet at them cottonwoods on the other side, so we can stand 'em off if they try to swim across after us."

That would have been a sure enough hot race if we had run it out, for we all four got as pretty a start as I ever see and went down the line all together with a bangin' of hoofs and Indian yells ringin' in our ears.

I glanced back, but, instead of seein' the boys in the midst of a decent retreat, the crowd was swarmin' after 'em like a nest of angry hornets, while Donnelley, with his reins between his teeth, was blazin' away at three reds who were right at Barrett's heels as he ran for his horse. Martin was lashin' his jumpin' cayuse away from the mob with sputtered and spit angry shots after him.

Hollis and I reached the river and crossed it half a mile ahead of the others and their yellin' bunch of trailers, so we were able to protect 'em in their crossin'.

I could see from their actions that Barrett and Martin was both hurt and I judged the deal hadn't panned out exactly accordin' to specifications.

The Crows didn't attempt to cross in the teeth of our fire, and the horses safely brought our comrades drippin' up the bank to where we lay takin' pot-shots at every bunch of feathers that approached the opposite bank.

We got Barrett's arm into a sling, and, as Martin's hurt wasn't serious, we lost no time in gettin' away.

"They simply beat us to it," complained Barrett, as we rode south. "You all had just started when young Long Hair grabs the money sack and ducks through the crowd, and the whole bunch turns loose on us at once."

"They got me, too, before I saw what was up," added Martin; "but I tore out of there like a jack-rabbit. Who'd a thought them durned Indians was dishonest enough for a trick like that?"

Then Donnelley spoke up and says: "Boys, as far as the coin goes, we're out an' injured; we just made a Mexican stand-off—lost our money, but saved our lives. What I want to know now is, how we're all goin' to get home, clean across the state of Texas, without a dollar in the outfit, and no assets but our guns and the nags."

That was a sure tough proposition. We'd bet every bean on that race. In them days there wasn't a railroad in that section, ranches were scatterin' and people weren't givin' pink teas to every stranger that rode up—especially when they were as hard-lookin' as we were.

"We've got to eat, and so's the horses," says Hollis, "but no ranchers is goin' to welcome with open arms as disreputable an outfit as we are. Two men shot up, and the rest of us without beddin', grub, money, or explanations. Them's what we need —explanations. What really happened just don't sound convincin', somehow. Everybody'll think some sheriff is after us, and two to one they'll put some Ranger on our trail, and we'll have more trouble. I believe I've had all I want for a while."

"I'll tell you how we'll work it," I says. "One of us'll be the sheriff of Guadalupe County, back home, with three deputies, bringin' back a prisoner that we've chased across the state. We'll ride up to a ranch an' demand lodgin' for ourselves and prisoner in the name of the state of Texas and say that we'll pay with vouchers on the county in the mornin'."

"No, sir! Not for me," says Martin. "I'm not goin' in for forgery. Our troubles'd only be startin' if we began that game."

"Your plan's all right, Kid," says Barrett to me. "You be the terrible desperado that I'm bringin' home after a bloody fight, where you wounded Martin and me, and almost escaped. You'll have ev'ry rancher's wife givin' you flowers and weepin' over your youth and kissin' you good-bye. In the mornin', when we're ready to go and I'm about to fix up the vouchers for our host, you break away and ride like the devil. We'll tear off a few shots and foller in a hurry, leavin' the farmer hopin' that the villain is recaptured and the girls tearfully prayin' that the gallant and misguided youth escapes."

It seemed to be about our only resort, as the country was full of bad men, and we were liable to get turned down cold if we didn't have some story, so we decided to try it on.

We rode up to a ranch 'bout dark, that night, me between the others, with my hands tied behind me, and Jim called the owner out of the ranch house.

"I want a night's lodgin' for my deputies and our prisoner," he says. "I'm the sheriff of Guadalupe County, and I'll fix up the bill in the mornin'."

"Come in! Come in!" the feller says, callin' a man for the horses. "Glad to accommodate you. Who's your prisoner?"

"That's Texas Charlie that robbed the Bank of Euclid single-handed," answers Jim. "He gave us a long run clean across the state, but we got him jest as he was gettin' over into the Indian Territory. Fought like a tiger."

It worked fine. The feller, whose name was Morgan, give us a good layout for the night and a bully breakfast next morning.

That desperado game was simply great. The other fellers attended to the horses, and I just sat around lookin' vicious, and had my grub brought to me, while the women acted sorrowful and fed me pie and watermelon pickles.

When we was ready to leave next morning, Jim says: "Now, Mr. Morgan, I'll fix up them vouchers with you." He gave me the wink, I let out a yell, and jabbin' the spurs into Black Hawk, we cleared the fence and was off like a puff of dust, with the rest of 'em shootin' and screamin' after me like mad.

Say! It was lovely—and when the boys overtook me, out of sight of the house, Morgan would have been astonished to see the sheriff, his posse, and the terrible desperado doubled up in their saddles laughin' fit to bust.

Well, sir! we never had a hitch in the proceedings for five days, and I was gettin' to feel a sort of pride in my record as a bank robber, forger, horse thief, and murderer, accordin' to the way Barrett presented it. He certainly was the boss liar of the range.

He had a story framed up that painted me as the bloodiest young tough the Lone Star had ever produced, and it never failed to get me all the attention there was in the house.

One night we came to the best-lookin' place we'd seen, and, in answer to Jim's summons, out walked an old man, followed by two of the prettiest girls I ever saw, who joined their father in invitin' us in.

"Glad to be of assistance to you, Mr. Sheriff," he said. "My name is Purdy, sir! Colonel Purdy, as you may have heard. In the Mexican War, special mention three times for distinguished conduct. These are my daughters, sir! Annabel and Marie."

As we went in, he continued, "You say you had a hard time gettin' your prisoner? He looks young for a criminal. What's he wanted for?"

Somehow, when I saw those girls blushin' and bowin' behind their father, I didn't care to have my crimes made out any blacker'n necessary and I tried to give Jim the high sign to let me off easy—just make it forgery or arson—but he was lookin' at the ladies, and evidently believin' in the strength of a good impression, he said:

"Well, yes! He's young, but they never was a old man with half his crimes. He's wanted for a good many things in different places, but I went after him for horse stealin' and murder. Killed a rancher and his little daughter, then set fire to the house and ran off a bunch o' stock."

"Oh! Oh! How dreadful!" shuddered the girls, backin' off with horrified glances at me.

I tried to get near Jim to step on his foot, but the old man was glarin' at me somethin' awful.

"Come to observe him closely, he has a depraved face," says he. "He looks the thorough criminal in every feature, dead to every decent impulse, I s'pose."

I could have showed him a live impulse that would have surprised him about then.

In those days I was considered a pretty handsome feller too, and I knew I had Jim beat before the draw on looks, but he continues makin' matters worse.

"Yes, and he's desperate too. One of the worst I ever see. We had an awful fight with him up here on the line of the Territory. He shot Martin and me before we got him. Ye see, I wanted to take him alive, and so I took chances on gettin' hurt.

"Thank ye, miss; my arm does ache considerable; of course, if you'd just as soon dress it—Oh, no! I'm no braver'n anybody else. I guess. Nice of ye to say so, anyhow." He went grinnin' out into the kitchen with the girls to fix up his arm.

The old man insisted on havin' my feet bound together and me fastened to a chair, and said: "Yes, yes, I know you can watch him, but you're in my house now, and I feel a share of the responsibility upon me. I've had experience with desperate characters and I'm goin' to be sure that this young reprobate don't escape his just punishment. Are you sure you don't need more help gettin' him home? I'll go with you if—"

"Thank ye," interrupted Hollis. "We've chased the scoundrel four hundred miles, and I reckon, now we've got him, we can keep him."

At supper, Jim, with his arm in a new sling, sat between the two girls who cooed over him and took turns feedin' him till it made me sick.

The old man had moved my chair up to the foot of the table and let Hollis bring me a plate of coarse grub after they all finished eatin'.

He had tied my ankles to the lower rung of the chair himself, and when I says to Hollis, "Those cords have plumb stopped my circulation, just ease 'em up a little," he went straight up.

"Don't you touch them knots!" the old man roared. "I know how to secure a man, and don't you try any of your games in my house, either, you young fiend. I'd never forgive myself if you escaped."

I ate everything I could reach, which wasn't much, and when I asked for the butter he glared at me and said: "Butter's too good for horse thieves; eat what's before you."

Every time I'd catch the eye of one of the girls and kind of grin and look enticing, she'd shiver and tell Jim that the marks of my depravity stood out on my face like warts on a toad.

Jim and the boys would all grin like idiots and invent a new crime for me. On the square, if I'd worked nights from the age of three I couldn't have done half they blamed me for.

After breakfast, when it came time to leave, Donnelley untied my feet and led me out into the yard, where the girls were hangin' around the colonel and Jim, who was preparin' to settle up.

As we rode up the evening before, I had noticed that we turned in from the road through a lane, and that the fence was too high to jump, so, when I threw my leg over Black Hawk, I hit Donnelley a swat in the neck, and, as he did a stage fall, I swept through the gate and down the lane.

The old man cut the halter off one of his Mexican warwhoops, and broke through the house on the run, appearin' at the front door with his shotgun just as I checked up to make the run onto the main road.

As I swung around, doubled over the horse's neck, he let drive with his old blunderbuss, and I caught two buckshot in my right arm where you see them marks.

I had sense enough to hang on and ride for my life, because I knew the old fire-eater would reckon it a pleasure to put an end to such a wretch as me, if he got half a chance.

I heard him howl, "Come on, boys! We'll get him yet," and, over my shoulder, I saw him jump one of his loose horses standin' in the yard and come tearin' down the lane, ahead of the befuddled sheriff and posse, his white hair streamin' and the shotgun wavin' aloft, as though chargin' an army at the head of his regiment.

From the way he drew away from the boys, I wouldn't have placed any money that he was wrong either.

I've always wondered how the old man ever got through that war with only three recommendations to the government.

He certainly kept good horses too, for in five minutes we'd left the posse behind, and I saw him madly urgin' his horse into range, reloadin' as he came.

As I threw the quirt into the mare with my good arm, I allowed I'd had about all the horse stealin' I wanted for a while.

The old devil finally saw he was losin' ground in spite of his best efforts, and let me have both barrels. I heard the shot patter on the hard road behind me, and hoped he'd quit and go home. But I'm blamed if he didn't chase me five miles farther before turnin' back, in hopes I'd cast a shoe or somethin' would happen to me.

I believe I was on the only horse in Texas that could have outrun the colonel and his that mornin'.

About noon I stopped at a blacksmith's shop, half dead with pain, and had my arm dressed and a big jolt of whiskey.

As the posse rode up to me, sittin' in the sun by the lathered flanks of my horse and nursin' my arm, Jim yells out: "Here he is! Surround him, boys! You're our prisoner!"

"No I'm blamed if I am," I says "You'll have to get another desperado. After this, I'm the sheriff."

*The primary characteristic of the novels and stories of B. M.
Bower (1871–1940) that made them so popular for close to
forty years is their realistic (and often quite funny) portrayal
of working cowboys on a large cattle ranch. This clear-cut
sense of realism surprises some when they learn that Bertha
Muzzy Bower was a woman; but she was born on one
Montana ranch, lived on another for most of her life, and
rode and roped with the best of the men. Her most accomplished fiction features the cowboys of the Flying U spread in
such novels as her first,* Chip of the Flying U *(1904), and
stories such as* "Bad Penny."

Bad Penny

B. M. Bower

The Flying U beef herd toiled up the last heartbreaking hill
and crawled slowly out upon the bench. Under the low-hanging
dust cloud which trailed far out behind, nothing much could be
seen of the herd save the big, swaying bodies and the rhythmi-
cally swinging heads of the leaders. Stolid as they looked,
steadily as they plodded forward under the eagle eye of the
point man, the steers were tired. Dust clogged blinking eye-
lashes, dust was in their nostrils, dust lay deep along their
backs. The boys on left flank rode with neckerchiefs pulled up
over their noses, yet they were not the most unfortunate riders
on the drive, for the fitful gusts of wind lifted the gray cloud occasionally and gave them a few clean breaths.

Back on the drag where the dust was thickest, the man they
called Penny choked, gasped, and spat viciously at the hind-
most steer. He pulled off a glove and rubbed his aching, blood-

38

shot eyes with bare fingertips, swearing a monotonous litany meanwhile, praying to be delivered from his present miseries and from any and all forms of cowpunching. Let him once live through this damnable day and he promised—nay, swore by all the gods he could name—that he'd chase himself into town and buy himself a barrel of whiskey and a barrel of beer and camp between the two of them until he had washed the dust out of his system.

Shorty, who was wagon boss during beef roundup for Jim Whitmore and had stopped half a mile back to gossip with a rancher out hunting his horses, galloped up in time to hear this last picturesque conception of a heaven on earth.

"Make it two barrels while you're about it," he advised unsympathetically. "You'll get 'em just as easy as you will a bottle." He laughed at his own humor—a thing Penny hated in any man—and rode on up to the point where he could help swing the herd down off the bench to the level creek bottom that was their present objective.

Penny renewed his cussing and his coughing and looked across at Chip Bennett, who was helping to push the tired drag along.

"You hear what that damn son-of-a-gun told me?" he called out. And when Chip nodded with the brief grin that he frequently gave a man instead of words, Penny swung closer. "You know what he done to me, don't yuh? Put me on day herd outa my turn—and don't ever think I don't see why he done it. So's I wouldn't get a chance to ride into town tonight. Gone temperance on me, the damn double-crosser. You heard him make that crack about me not gettin' a bottle uh beer, even? Runnin' a wagon has sure went to Shorty's head!"

"I don't think it's that altogether." Chip tried to soothe him. "You want to remember—"

Penny cut in on the sentence. "Remember what happened last time we shipped, I s'pose. Well, that ain't got nothin' to do with this time. I ain't planning to get owl-eyed this time and raise hell like I done before. I swore off three weeks ago, and Shorty knows it. I ain't had a drop fer three weeks."

Chip wheeled his horse to haze a laggard steer into line, and so hid his grin. Penny's swearing off liquor three weeks ago was a joke with the Flying U outfit. The pledge had followed a spree which no one would soon forget. For Penny had not only shot up the new little cow town of Dry Lake and stood guard in the street afterward watching for someone to show his nose outside—to be scared out of his senses by Penny's reckless shooting and his bloodcurdling war whoops—but he had been hauled to camp in the bed wagon next day, hog-tied to prevent his throwing himself out and maybe breaking his neck.

It was after he had recovered that he swore he never would touch another drop of anything stronger than Patsy's coffee. Those who had known him the longest laughed the loudest at that vow, and Shorty was one of them; though he, being lord of the roundup, had to preserve discipline and do his laughing in secret.

"It sure is tough back here," Chip conceded when the cattle were once more strung out and the two rode alongside again. "Cheer up, Penny. It'll be all the same a hundred years from now." And he added, when he saw signs of another outbreak in the grimed face of Penny, "Anyway, we'll all be in town tomorrow."

"If not before," Penny said darkly. "T'morra don't help me none right now." He whacked a dusty red steer into line with his quirt. "What grinds me is to have Shorty take the stand he does; slappin' me on herd outa my turn, like as if he was scared I might break out agin— Why, blast his lousy hide, I ain't got any idee of goin' in to town before t'morra when we load out. Er, I didn't have," he amended querulously. "Not till he went to work and shoved me on herd, just to keep me outa sight of the damn burg as long as he could." He stood in the saddle to ease the cramp in his legs. "Why, hell! If I wanted to go get me a snootful, it'd take more'n that to stop me!"

Still standing in the stirrups, he gazed longingly ahead over the rippling sea of dusty, marching cattle and swore again because the dust shut out the town from his straining sight. Miles away though it was, from this high benchland it would be clearly visible under normal conditions. The men on point could see the little huddle of black dots alongside the pencil line of railroad, he knew that.

"You know damn well, Chip," he complained, settling down off-center in the saddle so that one foot swung free, "that ain't no way to treat a man that's reformed and swore off drinkin'."

"Well, you don't have to stay back here on the drag eating dust," Chip pointed out. "Why don't you get up front awhile? You can probably see town if you ride point awhile, Penny. And another thing; you don't want to take this day-herding too personal. With Jack sick, somebody had to go on outa turn."

"Sick nothin'!" Penny snorted. "I know when a man's playin' off. Jack shore ain't foolin' me a damn bit. And, anyway, Shorty didn't have to go and pick on me."

Chip gave up the argument and swung back to bring up a straggler. Today they were not grazing the herd along as was their custom. The midsummer dry spell had made many a water hole no more than a wallow of caked mud, and most of the little creeks were bone dry. This was in a sense a forced drive, the day herders pushing the herd twice the usual distance ahead so that they would camp that night on the only creek for miles that had water running in it. That it lay within easy riding distance of town was what worried Penny.

Privately Chip thought Shorty had shown darned good sense in putting Penny on day herd. He'd have to stand guard that night—probably the middle guard, if he were taking Jack Bates's place—and that would keep him out of temptation, at least until after the cattle were loaded, when a little backsliding wouldn't matter so much. Whereas, had he been left to his regular routine, Penny would be lying around camp right now wishing he dared sneak off to town. He would have the short guard at the tail end of the afternoon, and at dusk he would have been relieved from duty until morning. With town so close it was easy to guess what Penny would have done with those night hours.

As it was, Penny would have no idle time save the two or three hours of lying around camp after the herd had been thrown on water. Then he'd have to sleep until he was called for middle guard. In the morning the whole outfit would be called out, and they'd be hard at it till the last steer was prodded into the last car and the door slid shut and locked. Then there would be more than Penny racing down to where they could wash the dust from their throats. No, Jack did get sick right at the exact time when it would keep Penny from getting drunk when he was most needed. A put-up job, most likely. Shorty wasn't so slow after all.

"We'll be down off the bench and on water in another hour," Chip yelled cheeringly when he came within shouting distance of Penny again.

Penny had turned sullen and he made no reply to that. He rode with both hands clasped upon the saddle horn, one foot swinging free of its stirrup, and a cigarette waggling in the corner of his mouth. His hat was pulled low over his smarting eyes, squinted half shut against the smothering dust that made his face as gray as his hat.

Not once during the remainder of the drive did he open his lips except when he coughed and spat out dust or when he swore briefly at a laggard steer. And Chip, being the tactful young man he was, let him alone to nurse his grudge. He did not sympathize with it, however, for Chip was still filled with a boyish enthusiasm for the picturesque quality of the drive. Even the discomfort of riding on the drag, with twelve hundred beef cattle kicking dust into his face, could not make him feel himself the martyr that Penny did.

For that reason and the fact that he never had felt the drunkard's torment of thirst, Chip certainly failed to grasp the full extent of Penny's resentment. He thought it was pretty cute of Shorty to fix it so that Penny couldn't get to town ahead of the herd. He had simply saved Penny from making seventeen kinds of a fool of himself and maybe kept him from losing his job as well. Let him sulk if he wanted to. He'd see the point when it was all over with and they were headed back onto the range again after another herd.

So they rode in the heat and the dust, each thinking his own thoughts. The herd plodded on in the scorching, windless heat, stepping more briskly as they neared the edge of the bench.

Bellowing thirstily, the cattle poured down the long, steep slope to the sluggish creek at the mouth of the narrow coulee. As the drag dipped down from the level, even Penny could see the long, level valley beyond and the little huddle of houses squatting against the farther hill. Two hundred yards up the creek and inside the coulee, the tents of the Flying U showed their familiar, homey blotches of gray-white against the brown grass. Behind them a line of green willows showed where the creek snaked away up the coulee. Never twice in the same setting, flitting like huge birds over the range to alight where water and feed were best, those two tents were home to the Flying U boys—a welcome sight when a long day's work was done.

Chip's eyes brightened at the sight, and he cleared his throat of the last clinging particles of dust. With a whoop he hailed the two men ambling out from camp to relieve them. Others would follow—were following even as he looked—to take charge of the tired, thirsty cattle already blotting the creek altogether from sight where they crowded to drink. Cal Emmett and Slim rode straight on to meet Chip and Penny.

"Gosh, ain't it hot!" Cal greeted them, voicing an obvious fact as is the way of men who have nothing important to say. "Weather breeder, if yuh ask me."

"Well, if it holds off till we get these cattle in the cars it can rain all it damn pleases," Chip replied carelessly. "I want to get caught up on my sleep, anyway."

"Don't you ever think it'll hold off! Bet you'll be huntin' buttons on your slicker tonight." Cal grinned. "Sure glad I don't have to stand guard t'night!"

"By golly, that's right," Slim agreed. "If it don't cut loose an' rain t'night I miss my guess."

Penny scowled at him, grunted, and rode on past. "Let 'er rain and be damned to it!" he muttered as he pricked his horse into a lope. But Chip had also put his horse into a gallop and failed to hear anything Penny might say.

At the rope corral as they rode up, Shorty was speaking to someone over across the *remuda*, judging from the pitch of his voice.

"No, sir! The man that rides to town before this beef is loaded can take his bed along with him. The cars'll be spotted sometime tonight, ready for us to start loadin' whenever we're ready tomorrow. I shore as hell ain't goin' to stop and round up a bunch of drunken punchers before I start workin' the herd in the mornin'."

Penny muttered an unprintable sentence as he dismounted and began loosening the *latigo*, and Chip gave him a quick questioning glance as he stepped down from his saddle close by. He glanced at Shorty, let his eyes go questing for the man he had been speaking to, and returned his glance to Penny.

"That's him every time, hittin' yuh over another man's back," Penny grumbled and shot an angry, sidelong glance at the wagon boss. "If he's got anything to say to me, why don't he spit it out to my face?"

"Ah, he wasn't talking to you," Chip protested, biting the words off short as Shorty turned and walked toward them.

The wagon boss gave them a sharp glance as he passed, almost as if he had overheard them. But he did not say anything and Penny did not look up.

Though other men chatted around him, Penny ate his supper in silence, scowling over his plate. Afterward he lay in the shade of the bed tent and smoked moodily until it was time to catch his night horse. No one paid any attention to him, for tempers were quite likely to be short at the end of a beef roundup, when sleep was broken with night-guarding a herd as temperamental as rival prima donnas are said to be and almost as valuable. If a man went into the sulks it was just as well to let him alone while the mood lasted. Which did not mean, however, that no one knew the state of mind he was in.

By the set of his head and the stiffness of his neck while he saddled his horse Penny proclaimed to his world that he was plenty mad. He looped up the long free end of the *latigo*, unhooked the stirrup from the horn, and let it drop with a snap that sent his horse ducking sidewise. He jerked him to a snorting stand, fixing a stern and warning eye upon him, hesitated just a second or two, and instead of tying him to the wagon as he should have done he jerked down his hat for swift riding, thrust his toe in the stirrup, and mounted.

"Here! Where you think you're goin'?" Shorty called out in surprise, leaping up from the ground.

"Goin' after my mail! Be right back." Penny grinned impudently over his shoulder as he wheeled his horse toward the open land. He was off, galloping down the coulee before Shorty could get the slack out of his jaw.

"His mail! Hell!" Shorty spluttered angrily, glaring after the spurts of dust Penny left behind him. "He ain't had a letter in all the two years I've knowed him." He stood irresolute, plainly tempted to give chase. Then he relaxed with a snort. "Think I'll hog-tie him and haul him out in the wagon again and sober him up?" he said disgustedly. "I'll fire the son-of-a-gun—"

Then he remembered that he was no longer just one of the Happy Family, free to speak his mind, but a full-fledged roundup foreman who had the dignity of his position to maintain. He stalked off to the cook tent and unrolled his bed, knowing full well that Penny would be howling drunk before midnight, and that by morning he would be unable to sit in the saddle—to say nothing of reading brands and helping work the herd and weed out strays before loading the cattle. The Flying U was already working shorthanded. He'd just have to consider himself shy another man, which went against the grain. Penny sober was a top hand—and, darn the luck, Shorty liked him.

He spread his blankets and started to get ready to crawl in, then decided that the air was too sultry inside and dragged his bed out under the mess wagon. Other men were deserting their canvas shelter in spite of the threatening clouds. For even at dusk the air was stifling. If it busted loose and rained they could move inside, but they'd be darned if they were going to suffocate in the meantime.

"Saddle yourselves a night horse before you turn in, boys." Shorty made a sudden decision as a whiff of cool air struck his face. "We can't take any chances at this stage of the game." And he went off to practice what he preached.

It was a sensible precaution, for if the storm did strike before morning there was no telling how bad it might be or how the herd would take it. Shorty had seen beef herds stampede in a thunderstorm and he hoped never to see another one—certainly not while he was responsible for the safety of the cattle. So, having done what he could to prepare for an emergency, Shorty crawled into his blankets and was snoring inside five minutes. And presently the dim bulks on the ground nearby were like-wise sleeping with the deep, unheeding slumber of work-weary men untroubled by conscience or care.

Down beyond the coulee mouth the night guard rode slowly round and round the sleeping herd. By sound they rode mostly, and by that unerring instinct that comes of long habit and the intimate knowledge it brings. As the sullen clouds crept closer it was so dark they could not see one another as they met and passed on. But the droning lullaby tones of their voices met and blended for a minute or so in pleasant companionship and un-derstanding. Then the voices would draw apart and recede into the suffocating blackness. The whisper of saddle leather, the mouthing of a bit, the faint rattle of bridle chains grew faint and finally were lost until, minutes later, the meeting came again.

Chip was young, and his imagination never slept. He liked the velvet blackness, the brooding mystery that descended upon the land with the dusk. Even the frogs over in the creek did their croaking tonight with bashful hesitation, as if they, too, felt the silence weigh upon them and only croaked because the habit was too strong for them. Chip thought of this breathless night as a curtained dome where some gigantic goddess walked and trailed her velvet robes, treading softly with her finger on her lips. Which only proves how young and imaginative he could be on night guard.

Away across the herd came the plaintive notes of a melan-choly song that Weary Willie seemed to favor lately, for no good reason save that it had many verses and a tune that lent it-self to melodious crooning. Chip hushed his own low singing to listen. In that breathless air, across twelve hundred sleeping steers, the words came clear.

> *"Oh, bury me not on the lone prairee*
> *Where the wild coyotes will howl o'er me,*
> *Where the rattlesnakes hiss and the wind blows free—*
> *Oh-h, bury me not on the lone prairee."*

Chip wondered who had written those words, anyway. Not a real cowboy, he'd bank on that. They'd sing it, of course, with that same wailing chorus plaintively making its sickish plea between the verses. But he didn't believe any real cowpuncher ever felt that way, when you came right down to it.

When a cowboy's light went out—according to the opinion of all the fellows he had ever heard discoursing on the subject—he didn't give a damn where they laid his carcass. They were quite likely to say, with unpleasant bluntness, "Just drag me off where I won't stink." But when they stood guard, like Weary tonight, nine times in ten they'd sing that maudlin old song. And though Chip would never admit it, over there in the dark the words lost their sickish sentimentality and seemed to carry a pulsing tremor of feeling.

> *"Oh, bury me where a mother's prayer*
> *And a sister's tears may linger there!*
> *Where my friends may come and weep o'er me—*
> *Oh, bury me not on the lone prairee!"*

In daylight Chip would have hooted at the lugubrious tones with which Weary Willie sang those words, but now he did not even smile to himself. The night like that and with sheet lightning playing along the skyline with the vague and distant mutter of thunder miles away, death and the tears and prayers of loved ones did not seem so incongruous.

> *"Oh, bury me not—but his voice failed there,*
> *And they gave no heed to his dying prayer.*
> *In a narrow grave just six by three-e,*
> *They-y buried him there on the lone prairee—"*

The singer was riding toward him, the soft thud of his horse's feet and the faint saddle sounds once more audible. A steer close to Chip blew a snorting breath, grunted and got to his feet, his horns rattling against the horns of his nearest neighbor. Chip forgot Weary and his song and began a soothing melody of his own. Another steer got up, and another. Black as it was, he sensed their uneasy, listening attitudes.

It couldn't have been Weary who wakened them. Weary had circled the herd many times with his melancholy ditty, his presence carrying reassurance. Chip dared not quicken his pace, dared not call a warning. Instead he began singing in his clear young tenor, hoping to override whatever fear was creeping on among the cattle.

> *"Come, love, come, the boat lies low—*
> *The moon shines bright on the old bayou—"*

Almost overhead the clouds brightened with the sudden flare of lightning, but the rumble that followed was slow and deep and need not have been disquieting to animals that had grown up in the land of sudden storms.

> *"Come, love, come, oh come along with me,*
> *I'll take you down-n to Tenn—"*

Off in the night there came the drumming of hoofs—some strange horseman coming at a swift gallop straight toward the herd. A chill prickled up Chip's neck. Slowly, carefully as a mother tiptoeing away from her sleeping baby, he reined aside and walked his horse out to meet and warn the approaching rider.

"Slow down!" he called cautiously when another lightning flare revealed the rider. "You'll be on top of the herd in another minute, you damn fool!"

A shrill, reckless yell from just ahead answered him: "Ayee-ee— Yipee! Them's the babies I'm a-lookin' for! Gotta stand guard! *Whee-ee!* Bossies, here's yer—what the hell?"

With an indescribable sound of clashing horns and great bodies moving in unison, the herd was up and away like flushed quail. There was no more warning than that first great swoosh of sound. Here and there steers bawled throatily— caught in the act of getting to their feet. Now they were battered back to earth as the herd lunged over them. For the cattle had taken fright on the outer fringe nearest camp and the open valley, and were stampeding across their own bed ground toward the bench.

The night was no longer silent under a velvety blackness. It was a roaring tumult of sound, the never-to-be-forgotten clamor of a stampede in full flight. Weary Willie, by God's mercy out of their path as he swung round the side toward the valley, yelled to Chip above the uproar.

"What started 'em? Y'all right, Chip?"

And Penny, with a pint or more of whiskey inside him and two quart flasks in his pockets, answered with another yell, "I did! Jus' sayin' hello—the damn things've fergot me a'ready!" He gave a whoop and emptied his six-shooter into the air as he galloped.

"Go it like hell!" he jeered, racing jubilantly after them. "Git a move on! *You* don't need no sleep, anyhow! What you want's—ex-ercise! Dammit, ex-ercise, you rip-pety-rip—" Cursing, laughing, shooting, he rode like a wild man, urging them on up and over the hill.

Up in camp Shorty lifted his head as the distant yelling came faint on the still air. Then came the shots and the vibrant roar of the stampede, but that was when Shorty had already jumped to his feet.

"Pile out!" he yelled. "The cattle's runnin'!"

Five words only, but they brought every man in camp out of his blankets, and grabbing for his clothes. Not much behind Shorty's hurried dressing they jerked on their boots, stamping their feet in on their way to their horses. They untied their mounts by the sense of touch alone, felt for stirrups in the inky blackness between lightning flashes, mounted, and were off, streaming down the coulee at a dead run. Even Patsy the cook was up and dressed and standing outside listening and swearing and trying to guess which way the cattle were running. Patsy had been almost caught in a stampede once when a herd had run past camp, and since then he took no chance if he could help himself.

To have a beef herd stampede in the night is a catastrophe at any time. To have it happen on the last night before they are crowded into cars and sent lurching away to market is next to the worst luck that can happen to a range man at shipping time.

The ultimate disaster, of course, would be to have the herd wiped out entirely.

Shorty looked at the clouds, quiet yet as approaching storms go, and wondered what had started the cattle. The shooting, he guessed, had been done in the hope of turning the herd. Then, above the fast decreasing rumble of the stampede, he heard a shrill yell he knew of old.

"Penny, by thunder!" He dug his heels into the flanks of his horse and swore aloud in his wrath. Certain broken phrases whipped backward on the wind he made in his headlong flight. "If I ever git my hands on the—" And again: "A man like him had oughta be strung up by the heels! —any damn fool that will go yellin' and shootin' into a beef herd bedded down—"

Shorty was not even aware that he was speaking. His horse stumbled over a loose rock, recovered himself with a lurch, and went pounding on across the creek and up the steep slope to the bench beyond. The horse knew and followed the sounds without a touch on the reins, would follow until he dropped or overtook the herd.

Around and behind him the riders were tearing along, their horses grunting as they took the steep hill in rabbit jumps. Good thing the cattle headed along the back trail, Shorty thought as his horse strained up the last bitter climb and lengthened his stride on the level. That hill would slow the herd down, maybe. Give the boys a chance to turn them. But with that drunken maniac still whooping up ahead, the prospect didn't look very bright.

On the left flank of the herd the night guard were racing, yelling, and shooting to turn the cattle. But they could not cover the unmistakable bellowing chant of Penny riding behind and to the right of the maddened herd and undoing the work of the left-flank boys. Shorty was so incensed that he actually turned that way with the full intention of overtaking Penny and shooting him off his horse. It seemed the only way to silence him. He didn't want to kill the cussed lunatic, but if he had to do it to shut him up no jury of range men would call it murder.

The storm clouds, too, were moving overhead, the lightning playing behind the tumbling thunderheads and turning them a golden yellow, with an occasional sword thrust of vivid flame.

But still the rain did not come down upon the thirsty land. The bulk of the storm, as Shorty saw with one quick backward glance, was swinging around to throw itself bodily against the rugged steeps of the mountains beyond.

Out upon the level, as the lightning brightened for an instant the whole landscape, they saw the herd a black blotch in the distance. With the cattle they glimpsed the night herders riding alongside the left flank, swinging the galloping herd more and more to the right. Of Penny they saw nothing. There was no more shooting, no more yelling.

"He's cooled down mighty sudden," Shorty gritted unforgivingly. "But that won't do him a damn bit of good when I get my hands on him. I'll sure as hell make him wish his mother'd been a man. He's through with this outfit, the rippety-rip—"

Away on the ragged fringe of the herd rode Chip and two other herders, with voices and swinging loops forcing the leaders around until they were running back the way they had come. As the bulk of the herd followed blindly where the others led, they too changed the course of their flight. In ten minutes or less the entire herd ran in a huge circle that slowed to a trot, then to a walk. "Milling," the cowboys called that uneasy circling round and round.

Within a mile or so the stampede was stopped, and except for one top hand forever disgraced and banished from the Flying U—and from the range, wherever the story seeped out—and a few broken-legged steers that would have to be shot, no harm had been done. The herd, at least, was intact. They had lost weight. Shorty would delay the shipping as long as he could hold the cars, to bring the cattle up to the best condition he could. A day, maybe—he'd ride in and see how much time he could have. Bad enough, but it could have been worse.

He rode over to where the lightning showed him Chip and Weary, meeting and halting a minute to compare notes and breathe their winded mounts.

"Good work, boys. Where's that—?" With as many unprintable epithets as he could string together he named the name of Penny.

"Search me, Shorty." Chip replied with a note of excitement still in his voice. "We dropped him right after we got out on the bench. He'd of had us clear down to the Missouri if he hadn't quit trying to shoot the tails off the drag. He's drunk as forty dollars.''

''He'll be sober when I git through with him,'' Shorty promised darkly. ''Bed the cattle right here if they'll settle down. Storm's goin' round us, I guess. You boys stand another hour and come on in. Have to double the guard from now till mornin'.''

''Hell, listen to that wind!'' Cal Emmett called out as he rode up. Men drew rein and turned in their saddles to look and listen. The clouds were thinning, drifting off to the north where the lightning jagged through the dark, but a great roaring came out of the nearer distance.

''That ain't wind,'' Shorty contradicted, and swung his horse around to stare at the inky blackness, until now utterly disregarded, in the east. ''It's comin' from off that way.'' And suddenly he jumped his horse into a run toward the valley. ''My God, it's water!'' he yelled as he rode, and all save the night guard, doubled now to six, followed him at top speed.

At the brink of the steep hillside they pulled up short and looked below. With the tremendous roaring in their ears they scarcely needed the flickering light of the distant storm or the feeble moon struggling through the clouds overhead. They could not see much, but they saw quite enough and they could guess the rest.

Down below, where the creek had meandered languidly through the willows, there was a solid, swirling wall of water. Down the coulee it pushed its resistless way, and they heard it go ravening out across the valley. The horses snorted and tried to bolt, though up there on the bench's rim they were safe. But where the herd had bedded for the night, down there beside the creek, there pushed a raging flood. Where the night hawk had taken the *remuda* none of them knew. Out into the valley, probably. If he heard and heeded he could run his horses to safety on high ground.

But the camp—''Patsy's caught!'' yelled Shorty, and reined his horse up along the hillside. They raced up the coulee side to where they could look down upon the camp—or where the camp had stood. A smooth brown plane of water flowed swiftly there, the willow tops trailing on the surface like the hair of drowned women.

No one mentioned Patsy again. Without a word they turned and rode back to the cattle. There was nothing else that they could do until daylight.

By sunrise the flood waters had passed on, and they rode down to search for the body of their cook and to retrieve what they could of the camp outfit. They passed the wagons, overturned and carried down to the mouth of the coulee where both had lodged in the bedraggled willows.

"We'll get them later on," said Shorty, and rode on. Without putting into words the thought in the minds of them all, they knew that Patsy came first.

He did. Waddling down the muddy flat with a lantern long burned dry, he met them with his bad news.

"Poys! Der vagon iss over!" he shouted excitedly as they rode up.

"Over where, Patsy?" Shorty asked gravely with a relieved twinkle in his eye.

"On his pack, you tamn fool!" snorted Patsy. "Der vater iss take him to hell and der stove mit. I cooks no preakfast, py tamn!"

They crowded around him, plying him with questions. Patsy, it appeared, had lighted the lantern and listened with both ears, ready to run if the cattle came up the coulee. The rush of water he had mistaken for the stampede coming, and he had run clumsily to the nearest coulee wall and climbed as high as he could. He had seen the wagons lifted and rolled over and carried off down the coulee. The demolition of the tents had not impressed him half so much, nor the loss of all their beds and gear.

There was nothing to do there, then. They rode back down the coulee hunting their belongings. One man was sent to town for grub and a borrowed outfit to cook it on, together with dishes and such. Hungry as when they had left the bench, the relief rode back to the herd.

Free for the moment, Chip started up the hill alone.

"Where yuh goin'?" Shorty yelled after him irritably, his nerves worn ragged with the night's mishaps.

"Going to find Penny." Chip yelled back. "You've cussed him and called him everything you could lay your tongue to—but it never seemed to occur to you that Penny saved the cattle—and a lot of your necks, too. What if you'd been asleep when that cloudburst—"

"Aw, don't be so damn mouthy!" Shorty cut him off. "I'll tend to Penny's case."

"Well, time you were doing it then," snapped Chip, just as if Shorty were still one of the boys with no authority whatever. "Me, I don't like the way he choked off his yelling so sudden, last night. I was on guard or I'd have looked for him then. The rest of you don't seem to give a damn."

"Now that'll be enough outa you." growled Shorty. "I guess I'm still boss around here." He spurred his horse up the hill and disappeared over the top.

And Chip, with Weary Willie at his heels as usual, followed him, grinning a little to himself.

"Mamma! You want to get yourself canned?" Weary protested as their horses climbed. "Shorty's went through a lot, remember."

"Well, he ain't through yet," replied Chip, grinning. "He'll go through a change of heart, if I ain't mistaken." And he added cryptically, "He's going to find Penny." And when Weary looked at him questioningly, he only shook his head. "I got there first, as it happens. On my way down. You wait."

So Shorty found Penny. He was lying almost as he fell when his horse stepped in a hole last night. Where the horse was now a systematic search might reveal; certainly he was nowhere in sight. A faint aroma of whiskey still lingered around the prone figure, but there were no bottles. Chip had seen to that.

Penny had a broken collarbone and an ear half torn off and one twisted ankle, but he was conscious and he managed to suppress a groan when Shorty piled off and knelt beside him.

"Yuh hurt, Penny?" A foolish question, but one invariably asked at such moments.

Penny bit back another groan. "The herd—did I git here—in time? Did I save—the cattle?" he murmured weakly, just as Chip had told him he must do.

"The cattle? Yeah, they're all right. Safe as hell, Penny. How—"

"Then—I got here—in time," muttered Penny, and went limp in his foreman's arms.

"And I was goin' to fire the son-of-a-gun!" said Shorty brokenly, looking up blur-eyes into Chip's face as he and Weary rode up.

Alan LeMay wrote many fine Western novels and short stories during the 1930s, 1940s, and 1950s, among them the classic chase novel, The Searchers, *which was filmed with John Wayne. "Trail Driver's Luck," the story of a cattle drive in Mexico and of a drover named Frazee, effectively captures all the drama and tension of cowboy life on the old frontier.*

Trail Driver's Luck

Alan LeMay

For a week the noise of the trail herd had beat steadily upon the ears of Frazee: by day a muffled rumble of hoofs, a sound deep and thick as a wrapping of hot cotton; by night an incessant dry bawling of thirst-tormented cattle. Now that he was away from the herd he noticed with surprise that the vast sunbaked levels of the Mexican plain still had a silence like the end of time, or the peace of God.

Yet there was an unrest under the silence, a small stir somewhere in the far northeast, up by the Texas border. So small was that irritant under the quiet that it could almost be forgotten, like a touch of cactus dust on the skin. Only when you listened carefully, unbreathing, could you be certain that to the northeast there were rifles popping, hundreds of them, in a straggling, shapeless battle.

That far-off rustle of gunpowder was very much in Frazee's mind, however, as he pulled up before the rancho of old Mario Contrera, just as the sun dropped behind the Sierra Madres.

The house of the Contrera rancho was long and commodious, and close to what ought to have been water; there were trees about it that had been set out long ago, and still lived, bent but mighty. Only the orchards behind had died utterly in the desert air. And only old Mario Contrera himself, who now came out of the house to speak to Frazee, was bent like the trees; a man who had had unusual height, but had lost it in the twist of the years. His mustache was as gray as if it had been full of alkali, and he had a bitter, furrowed face.

"Contrera?"

"*Si.*"

"My name's Frazee," said the rider. They spoke in Spanish. "Any water in your crick?"

"None."

"Nor any in—"

"Nor any place this side of the border itself."

Frazee shrugged, swearing silently. "There's clouds, though, there on the Sierras, Contrera."

"Always! Always!" Contrera's words burst out of him in passionate gusts. "All this devil's own summer, clouds hanging on the Sierras. But rain? Never! Never! And may God witness—" He paused, and made a hopeless gesture. "But—dismount, my friend. You must be thirsty and hungry."

"*Gracias.*"

A ragged boy took Frazee's horse, and the two men walked together to the house. "*Como se va?*" said Frazee, flicking his eyes northeast.

Contrera was in no doubt as to what Frazee meant. What should anyone be asking about but the progress of the revolt? A dark emotion twisted old Mario's face as definitely as if it had been gripped by a hand.

"Esparza stands like a bull. He still holds Ojo Caliente."

"Good!"

"You favor the revolt?"

"I favor Cherry Frazee," said the rider harshly, indicating himself. He chuckled, but in a way that Contrera perhaps did not like. "That dust—there in the southeast—my cattle are raising that. Five thousand damned gaunt, black-tongued, low-horned head! That is—they were five thousand three days ago. Naturally, we're losing a few."

"I heard of your purchase, señor. And your drive up from Las Lomas. A valiant effort, my friend! I sympathize deeply."

"Sympathize?"

"This hell's own frying pan sucks the life out of cattle as if they were tadpoles, this year," said Contrera. "And to drive across it a starved and weakened herd—!"

Frazee laughed harshly. "I'll put them over the border in four days. And then—I've got hay at Loring, held for me until the tenth of August. Hay and water will fix 'em up."

"Ah, Loring," said Contrera. His voice suggested that Loring was two miles beyond doomsday, as far as Frazee's cattle were concerned. "The cows are strong? You have plenty of men?"

"The cattle can hardly stand; I have two men with me, and loafers at that!"

Contrera tossed up his hands.

Frazee grinned. It had taken all he had, and all his credit, to tie up hay at Loring, and to buy—even for a song—a drought-punished herd deep down in old Mexico. This, however, was the sort of battle with urgency that he liked and was made for. Long chances were his natural roads to fortune, punishment his meat.

Contrera stood aside to let Frazee precede him through a cool, dark hall to an inner patio where the earth was kept firm and dustless by the water it drew up—and wasted—from an enormous cistern in the middle.

A girl was standing by the cistern head. Instantly, before he saw her face at all, Frazee knew who this was. He would have known the shadow of her shadow in hell, by just the bend of her head. The recognition took effect upon Frazee with a curious sense of shock; and immediately a small world of memories rushed through him like a flood released—so swift, yet so complete, as to be less a recollection than an emotion.

Francisca Contrera must have pretended not to hear them, for had she heard their approach it would have been her duty to remove herself from the patio. Young Spanish women did not receive chance strangers, under the reign of the old ways. But Frazee knew women well enough to know that she had proba-

bly watched him ride up from a long way off. All that went
through his head when he first saw her standing by the cistern
head, her face turned away.

But that was in the background, a shadow. The important
thing was that he had once held this girl in his arms, and kissed
her well enough to make her remember him, once and for all.
That had been at a fiesta that he had crashed at Monte Solano
two years—three years ago, it must have been.

It had been a hard job, that day three years ago, to get a moment with her alone. So heavily chaperoned were those upper-
class Spanish girls that few would have tried it. But Frazee had
achieved perhaps three minutes alone with the girl in a shadowed walk that passed between a chapel and a clump of bam-
boo, and before her duenna had come seeking her he had seen
all her pretended aloofness melt within the pressure of his arms.

Now, as she met his eyes for an instant in her father's patio,
he saw the blood come into her face, and knew that she had had
the same instant memory as he.

"Francisca," said Contrera, "let me present Señor Frazee—a drover." The last two words exploded ill-temperedly,
telling Frazee that the introduction itself was intended as a re-
buke. "My daughter," he said to Frazee with the same dry-
ness. "We will excuse you, Francisca."

As she left them she sent Frazee a glance full of laughter,
such as some women use to tease men who have had some
small part of their favor, but will have no more. But what Frazee got out of it was a sudden conviction that he should have
found out who she was, and searched her out again long ago.
Until today, though he had remembered her often, he had never
known her name.

A small wizened priest—or was it a friar?—in a brown robe and
an incongruous little stiff-brimmed straw hat, joined them as
Contrera provided wine, and presently food. After the inevita-
ble peppered beans and meat there was white tequila, and with
the closing of the hot dark Contrera became a little more expan-
sive. As the old rancher monotoned the history of his misfor-
tunes, what with repeated war and everlasting drought, Frazee

found that he sat stark awake, where he would have expected to drowse. He had glimpsed a white mantilla at a patio window, and knew that Francisca's eyes were upon him: and when this was gone he remained intensely conscious of the girl's presence in the house. He was listening and waiting, without knowing what for.

Mario Contrera seemed to be waiting also. Behind the old man's monotone was an edge, as if he knew that something was about to happen, or that some word was to arrive that was going to change the meaning of everything on that hot, dry plain. Yet, when that word came, it was Frazee who was the more openly affected.

A rider, a blunt-faced, swarthy man with Indian eyes, dropped off his horse before the outer door; and when he was admitted he stood fumbling his hat before Contrera.

"Señor"—the messenger's word rattled like machine gunnery—"Esparza breaks! He falls back. His cavalry is God knows where. Ojo Caliente falls; he is beaten out of it. The army of the people is strung out for fifteen miles, and whoever is last, that is the rear guard, can protect themselves as they can. They say he cannot rally at the Moro as was thought; they say he will not stand now until Boleros; and if God does not strike over his shoulder there, it is done. They say—"

"You're sure of this?"

"Señor, I myself rode among the—"

"How far is the retreat from Ojo Caliente?" Frazee demanded.

"*No lejos.*" That was the Mexican measurement: far, or not far. It might mean a day's march or a mile.

"Will the advance reach Boleros tomorrow night?"

"Señor, no! I am only here because I rode like the cinders of hell. Esparza—"

"In two days, then?"

"As God wills."

Frazee smashed a furious fist down upon the table, and smoking words rumbled in his throat.

"Loring will never see the cattle of Frazee, señor," said Contrera with weary amusement. "In two days—three—there will be a twenty-mile wall of starving soldiery between. It is confiscation, señor!''

"They'll have to come fast, then," swore Frazee. "I'm a long shot nearer Boleros than he is, and once my herd point sets hoof—"

"I understand your cattle could hardly stand up," said Contrera.

"By God, I'll hold 'em up if I have to tail 'em up! If that herd stops here it'll die where it stands. If only I had twenty—"

"I have not a man to spare you," Contrera forestalled him.

Frazee's ears still drummed with the beating shuffle and bawl of that low-headed, spraddle-legged herd of his. To bring that herd to feed and water was to send his fortunes rocketing; to fail in this or to walk into confiscation at Boleros was to lose everything he had. The chance had been a slender one to begin with, and the odds were multiplying against him; yet, inarticulately, a sense of approaching triumph was upon him.

"I tell you this," said Frazee, his voice low and harsh. "Everything I have is in that herd of cattle. As you say, I cannot drive cattle through a rout of starving men. But if I'm first to Boleros, if I get that herd to the border—"

"I have not a man to spare you," said Contrera again. "I'm sorry, my friend."

Frazee relaxed and grinned.

"Bueno," he said. "I have only two men, and those worthless; but I'll put four thousand of those five thousand head over the line!"

"Three men, with half-dead cattle, reach Boleros before Esparza? Impossible!"

"You'll see it done before the week's out."

Contrera shivered. "It's time for sleep," he said wearily. "A man is lucky to have a bed, and a roof over it, in times like these."

Alone in the little cell-like room assigned him, Frazee stood looking out of the window. The brush-dotted plain lay flat and silent under hot, brassy stars, and the Madres were lost in the dark. The broken whisper beyond the northeast horizon seemed stronger now.

The yammer of a coyote drowned the ragged murmur of the distant guns, and he turned away. Slowly he stripped, and sponged himself with tepid water from an earthen jar. Slowly also he pulled on his dusty clothes. He meant to be gone from there long before dawn.

Then suddenly he became acutely conscious again that the girl was somewhere near at hand, in the same household, under the same roof. She had been partly eclipsed, for a little while, by the necessities of his low-headed herd; but now his mind filled with her so completely that he could not stretch out on his bed, nor attempt sleep.

He considered the layout of the rancho; and what he instantly pictured was the dry, withered orchard, divided by the dry serpentine bed of the river that had failed the trees.

Frazee stepped to his window. It was set with bars, but the first one that he tried cracked in his grip. Those bars must have been eaten into shells by the dry rot, for three or four of them almost went to dust as he broke them out with his hands, and stepped out into the open starlight of the plain.

Quiet-footed, he walked where the brown-leafed willows stood hot and lonely under the stars, marking the course of the waterless river. Then his eyes found a gleam of white, and he grinned, and the night was lonely no more.

In spite of his assurance, his certainty of himself, he had less than half expected that she would really be there. Yet she was there, waiting for him just as certainly as if it had been prearranged.

"*Buenas noches,*" she murmured, her voice faintly cordial. "What are you doing here?"

"Came out to talk to you," he said.

"And who asked you to do that—drover?"

"Now, pish, tush," said Frazee. He took her arm, and clamped it against his side; and though she stiffened she walked a little way farther from the house with him before she broke away.

"What was it you wanted to say?" the girl asked.

"I've been looking for you for three years," Frazee heard himself lie. "I don't know as you've been out of my mind an hour. And now, I've run on to you again, I don't mean to leave you go."

She smiled up at him sidelong, queerly. "What do you mean by that?"

"I'm going to marry you."

They stood silent; and the lonely Mexican night pressed nearer to them, hot and close. Then she looked at him curiously, and the cool poise seemed to go out of her. She began to laugh, almost silently, in her throat.

"What are you laughing at?" he demanded hotly.

"I was thinking of José."

"Who's José?"

"Did you ever see a man named José Exnicios?"

"No."

"I'm going to marry him the tenth of August. We leave for the south in three days."

"The hell you are!"

"Why am I not?"

"Because before those three days are up I'm coming after you. And you'll be ready to come with me, and you'll come with me—you hear?"

"And if I don't?"

"Then I'll take you; and I tell you this: it'll take more than the army of Mexico, and all hell, and you yourself to stop me."

A strange-voiced exclamation sounded startlingly, very close at hand: the breathy cry of an old man who comes sharply upon unutterable horror. Frazee, jerking up his head, saw the withered padre, shadowless and vague in the starlight. Then Francisca spoke.

"Padre," she began, her low voice unexpectedly clear and cool, "before you speak, before you judge—"

The robed figure stirred as if released from a spell. "You had better go in, my child."

Francisca obeyed. But first she leaned close for half a second to Frazee, speaking to him in a desperate whisper: "Within three days?"

"Depend on me."

Shortly after daylight he found his herd, bedded eleven miles east of the Contrera rancho. That day Frazee did the work of three, changing horses at noon. His good vaqueros had deserted him for the fortunes of war—and his two remaining riders did little work, and that sullenly.

To see that every beast of that bawling, stumbling ruck moved steadily, never hurried, yet never lagging nor wandering aside, would have been an insuperable job for many more men than Frazee; but it meant the difference between failure and success. He swarmed at it like a man inspired, a grim, grinning glow in his reddened eyes as he worried the stragglers. The whisper of rifle fire was stronger now, but still far to the east; and a faint haze on the horizon showed him where Boleros lay. He had never been surer in his life that he was close to a great victory. One day more . . .

One day more to pass Boleros. Then the next day the two punk riders could muddle the herd along as best they could, for the chief danger would be past. That would leave Frazee free to kill a horse returning to the Contrera rancho for the girl. Francisca would be with him on the last short day, while they pressed the herd across the border to Loring, the goal that had been ahead of him for so long.

In a sense she was with him already. All that day they plugged across Contrera lands, and somehow that knowledge made her seem closer; as if her presence followed with him, like the sun.

Then, late in the afternoon, an Indian boy came riding a paint pony out of the southwest, whipping up side-and-side with his tie rope as he came in sight of the herd. He handed Frazee a tiny, twisted wad of paper.

When Frazee had smoothed the paper out he still had to stop his horse before he could decipher, with difficulty, the hesitant, sketchy little scrawl of three words that it contained.

"Never after tonight—"

"The señorita?" he demanded.

"*Si,* señor."

"And what does she say?"

"Nothing, señor."

"You don't know what she wants, or anything about it, but just this fool wad of paper?"

"Nothing, señor."

"What night is she talking about?"

A blank stare was all he got out of that.

"Then—go hump that far bunch back into the show—pick 'em up, pick 'em up, but easy, see, or I break your—"

"*Si,* señor!"

Never after what night? Last night? If it was that, he could call it meaningless. But if never after *this* night— Never what after when?

If Francisca had only had the sense to— But he knew that there was purpose in the ambiguity of those three words. She had to guard against interception, and so had written what should be meaningless to anyone but him. Ironically, it was also meaningless to Frazee. But she had sent for him, he was pretty sure of that; and if she sent for him she had a reason. . . .

He wasted a futile moment reestimating the two riders who held the point to its trail—two men of not much guts, sick and disgusted long ago with what they felt was a hopeless job. He knew with utter certainty that those two would never attempt to work the herd through for him alone, or succeed if they tried. If Frazee left the herd here those worn-out cattle would scatter where they stood, to die presently in the unrelenting drought.

"Never after tonight—"

Suddenly he saw that he was at the end of something. One thing or the other was over and done with.

He sat motionless on the stopped horse, watching the mile-long straggle that the herd had become. They plugged along unevenly, a long welter of gaunt backs under a haze of dust. There in the slow hoofs of the cattle walked fortune. That herd was the tide which, "taken at the flood . . ." Frazee himself was the very soul of that tide, the heart and guts of it that walked it on—as much as part of it as it was of him. And though his teeth were set hard into victory the odds were heavy against him yet, and that was hardest of all; for the grip of utter urgency that was upon that herd held him with an all but resistless appeal.

The straggling tail of the herd passed him now, plodding doggedly with swinging heads. And finally the last gaunt cow, a staggering calf at her flank, passed and drew away from him slowly, slowly, as fortune was slipping out of his grasp.

He began to laugh, cracking his dry lips. This was the turning point of his career; yet he found himself without hesitation or doubt. Jauntily he kissed his hand to the herd, and unbuckled his chap strap to get at his money belt beneath. Then he signaled his riders in.

It was not long after starlight when Frazee, leading an extra horse, came within sight of the Contrera rancho again.

He sent the Indian boy ahead to see if anyone was up, and if possible to tell Francisca that Frazee was here. Then, while waiting at a distance, a strange fear lay cold across his shoulders, so ghastly pale and dead that house looked under the stars.

The boy was gone a long time, more than an hour, it seemed to Frazee. He came slinking out at last, so nearly invisible in the little light that Frazee did not see him until he was very close.

"The señorita—?"

"I don't know."

"See anyone?"

"No one, señor. *El padre*. I saw the padre. He saw me, too, but I didn't want to talk to him. I ran out of his way."

"In hell's name, what took you all this time?"

"I looked all over. The horses are gone from the stable."

"Horses? What horses?"

"All the family horses, the kept-at-the-house horses: though there is stock in the corral that—"

Frazee swung into his saddle and put the pony to the house at a run. At the heavy front door he knocked twice, but when nothing moved within he ran around the house to the window of his room of the night before. Here he entered through the broken window bars, and went striding on into the patio.

The ubiquitous little padre was sitting by the cistern head, a lantern beside his feet.

"You, old man—where's Francisca?"

The padre's voice shot back at him, unexpectedly harsh and sharp. "And who knows if you don't?"

"What do you mean? Do you mean to say she's—"

"Her family left this morning—Contrera changed his plans for reasons that you should know best. But before they left, the señorita—she was gone."

"Gone where?"

"It's supposed," said the padre almost savagely, "that you took her!"

"So the family—"

"They thought you had ridden south; naturally you wouldn't try to rejoin your herd under their very noses. They have gone southward in pursuit."

"Padre, listen: I never took her! I don't know anything about it!"

"You swear it?"

"Sure I swear it!"

The little old man stood staring at Frazee with eyes like lancets. "What has happened here, then?" he mumbled dimly.

Frazee seized the old man by the shoulders as if he would shake his brain awake. "Think, padre: where could she go? What could happen to her here?"

"I don't know . . . I don't know. . . ."

A silence fell upon them, as complete as if the world had turned still as the sky. Then softly, somewhere in a far wing of the house, Frazee heard a door open and close.

He snatched up the lantern and went running into the shadows of the still house, not calling out, but with quiet feet, trying to listen as he went.

In her own room, on her knees beside her bed, he found Francisca. She seemed afraid of him now, and hid her face; but when he gathered her up in his arms she buried her face in his shoulder and wept.

"Child, what's happened?"

"I wouldn't go south with them, I wouldn't go—but I had to trick them. I hid my saddle, and myself with it, and they thought I was gone. They're looking for me—and you—in Monte Solano, by now, I suppose. I knew you'd come. But you took a long time. . . ."

The padre came, following the lantern light, his slippers slop-slopping on the floor tiles. Francisca freed herself from Frazee's arms and stood quiet, facing the robed old man—tall and serene, and certain of herself, like a young-faced madonna; except that there was an unmadonnalike smoldering fire behind the surface of her eyes.

"You are about to marry us, padre," said Frazee.

"But if that is impossible?"

"Then, by God, I'll take her anyway!"

"But—if—"

"And I'll go with him," said Francisca.

The padre regarded them with miserable eyes. Then, "Stand here before the cross," he said at last. . . .

"Where's your saddle?" Frazee asked when the padre was gone.

He could hardly hear her answer, her voice had turned so shaky and faint. "There's no need . . . Isn't this our house to-night?"

Waking a short hour before dawn, Frazee strained his eyes against such blackness as he could not remember having seen before. There were no longer stars beyond the window bars; but the night had lost its silence, and the whole of the vast desert was filled with a new rush and moan of sound that at first he could not believe.

Gently he drew his arm from under Francisca's sleeping head; but once clear he reached the window in a bound. A slash of water struck in through the jalousie and whipped wet across his face, bringing him broad awake. For an instant more he stood incredulous; then with one sweep of his arm he knocked the rotted shutter out of the way, and stepped out into the downpour.

He spread out his arms to it, prayerfully letting the mild, big-dropped deluge run down his body in rivulets and paste his hair down into his eyes. He was picturing to himself his wet-backed herd thirstily sucking up the saving water from rivulets and swales. She was sure enough his luck, luck past all believing! If he had pushed on, into the path of that hard-pressed retreat—

In the whir and slat of the rain he was hearing the shuffle of numberless hoofs; and he knew that he was listening to prophecy, the rain's promise to him of mighty herds unborn.

Theodore Sturgeon has written relatively little Western fiction—one novel, The Rare Breed *(1966), based on the screenplay for the film starring James Stewart and Maureen O'Hara; and several short stories for* Zane Grey Western Magazine *in the late 1940s and early 1950s. The best of his short stories, some in collaboration with Don Ward, were collected in* Sturgeon's West *(1973). And perhaps the best of all of them is ''Scars,'' a masterful tale about a cowboy named Kellet and his act of kindness. Its surprising last line is one you won't soon forget.*

Scars

Theodore Sturgeon

There is a time when a thing in the mind is a heavy thing to carry, and then it must be put down. But such is its nature that it cannot be set on a rock or shouldered off on to the fork of a tree, like a heavy pack. There is only one thing shaped to receive it, and that is another human mind. There is only one time when it can be done, and that is in a shared solitude. It cannot be done when a man is alone, and no man aloof in a crowd ever does it.

Riding fence gives a man this special solitude until his throat is full of it. It will come maybe two or three weeks out, with the days full of heat and gnats and the thrum of wire under the stretcher, and the nights full of stars and silence. Sometimes in those nights a chunk will fall in the fire, or a wolf will howl, and just then a man might realize that his partner is awake too, and that a thing in his mind is growing and swelling and becoming heavy. If it gets to be heavy enough, it is put down softly, like fine china, cushioned apart with thick strips of quiet.

That is why a wise foreman pairs his fence riders carefully. A man will tell things, sometimes, things grown into him like the calluses from his wire cutters, things as much a part of him, say, as a notched ear or bullet scars in his belly; and his hearer should be a man who will not mention them after sun-up—perhaps not until his partner is dead—perhaps never.

Kellet was a man who had calluses from wire cutters, and a notched ear, and old bullet scars low down on his belly. He's dead now. Powers never asked to hear about the scars. Powers was a good fence man and a good partner. They worked in silence, mostly, except for a grunt when a post-hole was deep enough, or "Here," when one of them handed over a tool. When they pitched for the night, there was no saying "You get the wood," or "Make the coffee." One or the other would just do it. Afterward they sat and smoked, and sometimes they talked, and sometimes they did not, and sometimes what they said was important to them, and sometimes it was not.

Kellet told about the ear while he was cooking one evening. Squatting to windward of the fire, he rolled the long-handled skillet deftly, found himself looking at it like a man suddenly scanning the design of a ring he has worn for years.

"Was in a fight one time," he said.

Powers said, "Woman."

"Yup," said Kellet. "Got real sweet on a dressmaker in Kelso when I was a bucko like you. Used to eat there. Made good mulligan."

They were eating, some ten minutes later, when he continued. " 'Long comes this other feller, had grease on his hair. He shore smelt purty."

"Mexican?"

"Easterner."

Powers's silence was contributory rather than receptive at this point.

"She said to come right in. Spoons him out what should be my seconds o' stew. Gets to gigglin' an' fussin' over him." He paused and chewed, and when the nutritious obstacle was out of the way, spat vehemently. "Reckon I cussed a little. Couldn't he'p m'self. Next thing you know, he's a-tellin' me what language not to use in front of a lady. We went round and round together and that ended quick. See this ear?''

''Pulled a knife on you.''

Kellet shook his big, seamed head. ''Nup. She hit me a lick with the skillet. Tuk out part o' my ear. After, it tuk me the better part of an hour with tar soap to wash the last o' that hair grease offen my knuckles.''

One bullet made the holes in his stomach, Kellet told Powers laconically while they were having a dip in a cold stream one afternoon.

''Carried a leetle pot-belly in them days,'' said Kellet. ''Bullet went in one side and out t'other. I figgered fer a while they might's well rack me, stick me, bleed me, and smoke me fer fall. But I made it. Shore lost that pot-belly in th' gov'ment hospital, though. They wouldn't feed me but custards and like that. My plumbin' was all mixed up an' cross-connected.

''Feller in th' next bed died one night. They used t'wake us up 'fore daybreak with breakfast. He had prunes. I shore wanted them prunes. When I see he don't need 'em I ate 'em. Figgered nobody had to know.'' He chuckled.

Later, when they were dressed and mounted and following the fence, he added, ''They found the prune stones in m' bandages.''

But it was at night that Kellet told the other thing, the thing that grew on like a callus and went deeper than bullet scars.

Powers had been talking, for a change. Women. ''They always got a out,'' he complained. He put an elbow out of his sleeping bag and leaned on it. Affecting a gravelly soprano, he said, ''I'd like you better, George, if you'd ack like a gentleman.''

He pulled in the elbow and lay down with an eloquent thump. ''I know what a gentleman is. It's whatever in the world you cain't be, not if you sprouted wings and wore a hello. *I* never seen one. I mean, I never seen a man yet where *some* woman, *some* time, couldn't tell him to ack like he was one.''

The fire burned bright, and after a time it burned low. ''I'm one,'' said Kellet.

Powers then sensed that thing, that heavy growth of memory.

He said nothing. He was awake, and he knew that somehow Kellet knew it.

Kellet said, "Know the Pushmataha country? Nuh—you wouldn't. Crick up there called Kiamichi. Quit a outfit up Winding Stair way and was driftin'. Come up over this little rise and was well down t'ord th' crick when I see somethin' flash in the water. It's a woman in there. I pulled up pronto. I was that startled. She was mother-nekkid.

"Up she goes on t'other side 'til she's about knee-deep, an' shakes back her hair, and then she sees me. Makes a dive fer th' bank, slips, I reckon. Anyway, down she goes an' lays still.

"I tell you, man, I felt real bad. I don't like to cause a lady no upset. I'd as soon wheeled back and fergot the whole thing. But what was I goin' to do—let her drown? Mebbe she was hurt.

"I hightailed right down there. Figured she'd ruther be alive an' embarrassed than at peace an' dead.

"She was hurt all right. Hit her head. Was a homestead downstream a hundred yards. Picked her up—she didn't weigh no more'n a buffalo calf—an' toted her down there. Yipped, but there wasn't no one around. Went in, found a bed, an' put her on it. Left her, whistled up my cayuse, an' got to m' saddlebags. When I got back she was bleedin' pretty bad. Found a towel for under her head. Washed the cut with whiskey. Four-five inches long under the edge of her hair. She had that hair that's black, but blue when the sun's on it."

He was quiet for a long time. Powers found his pipe, filled it, rose, got a coal from the dying fire, lit up, and went back to his bedroll. He said nothing.

When he was ready, Kellet said, "She was alive, but out cold. I didn't know what the hell to do. The bleedin' stopped after a while, but I didn't know whether to rub her wrists or stand on m' head. I ain't no doctor. Finally I just set there near her to wait. Mebbe she'd wake up, mebbe somebuddy'd come. Mebbe I'd have my poke full o' trouble if somebuddy did come—I knowed that. But what was I goin' to do—ride off?

"When it got dark two-three hours later I got up an' lit a tallow-fat lamp an' a fire, an' made some coffee. Used my own Arbuckle. 'Bout got it brewed, heard a funny kind of squeak from t'other room. She's settin' bolt upright lookin' at me through the door, clutchin' the blanket to her so hard she like to push it through to t'other side, an' makin' her eyes round's a hitchin' ring. Went to her an' she squeaked ag'in an' scrambled away off into the corner an' tole' me not to touch her.

"Said, 'I won't, ma'am. Yo're hurt. You better take it easy.'

" 'Who are you?' she says. 'What you doin' here?' she says.

"I tol' her my name, says, 'Look, now yo're bleedin' ag'in. Just you lie down, now, an' let me fix it.'

"I don't know as she trusted me or she got faint. Anyway, down she went, an' I put a cold cloth on the cut. She says, 'What happened?'

"Tole her, best I could. Up she comes ag'in. 'I was bathin'!' she says, 'I didn't have no—' And she don't get no further'n that, just squeaks some more.

"I says, straight out, 'Ma'am, you fell an' hurt yore head. I don't recall a thing but that. I couldn't do nought but what I did. Reckon it was sort of my fault, anyway. I don't mean you no harm. Soon's you git some help I'll leave. Where's your men-folks?'

"That quieted her down. She tole me about herself. She was homesteadin'. Had pre-emption rights an' eighteen months left t' finish th' term. Husband killed in a rock-slide. Swore to him she'd hold th' land. Didn't know what she'd do after, but spang shore she was a-goin' to do that first. Lot o' spunk."

Kellet was quiet again. The loom of the moon took black from the sky and gave it to the eastward ridge. Powers's pipe gurgled suddenly.

"Neighbor fourteen mile downstream was burned out the winter before. Feller eight mile t'other way gone up to Winding Stair for a roundup, taken his wife. Be gone another two months. This little gal sweat out corn and peas for dryin', had taters put by. Nobuddy ever come near, almost. Hot day, she just naturally bathed in the crick.

"Asked her what about drifters like me, but mebbe gunmen. She reached under the bed, drug out a derringer. Says, 'This's for sech trash.' An' a leetle pointy knife. 'This's for me,' she says, just like that. I tol' her to keep both o' 'em by her. Was that sorry for her, liked her grit so, I felt half sick with it.

"Was goin' to turn in outside, by the shed. After we talked

some an' I made her up some johnny-cake, she said I c'd bunk in th' kitchen if I wanted. Tol' her to lock her door. She locked it. Big wooden bar. I put down m' roll an' turned in.''

The moon was a bead on the hill's haloed brow; a coronet, then a crown.

Powers put his pipe away.

''In th' mornin','' said Kellet, ''she couldn't get up. I just naturally kicked the door down when she wouldn't answer. Had a bad fever. Fast asleep an' couldn't wake up but for a half minute, an' then she'd slide off ag'in. Set by her 'most all day, 'cept where I saw to my hoss an' fixed some vittles. Did for her like you would for a kid. Kept washin' her face with cold water. Never done nothin' like that before; didn't know much what to do, done the best I could.

''Afternoon, she talked for an hour or so, real wild. Mostly to her man, like he was settin' there 'stead o' me. He was a lucky feller. She said . . .

''Be damned to you what she said. But I . . . tuk to an-swerin' her oncet in a while, just 'Yes, honey,' when she got to callin' hard for him. Man a full year dead, I don't think she really believed it, not all the way down. She said things to him like—like no woman ever thought to say to me. Anyway . . . when I answered thataway she'd talk quiet. If I didn't she'd just call and call, and git all roiled up, an' her head would bleed, so what else you expect me to do?

''Next day she was better, but a weak's a starveling colt in a blowin' drought. Slept a lot. I found out where she's been jer-kin' venison, an' finished it up. Got some weeds outen her black-eye peas. Went back ever' now an' then to see she's all right. Remembered some red haw back over the ridge, rode over there and gathered some, fixed 'em to sun so's she'd have 'em for dried-apple pie come winter.

''Four-five days went by like that. Got a deer one day, skinned it an' jerked it. Done some carpenterin' in th' shed an' in th' house. Done what I could. Time I was fixin' th' door to th' kitchen I'd kicked down that first mornin', she lay a-watchin' me an' when I was done, she said I was good. 'Yo're good, Kellet,' she said. Don't sound like much to tell it. Was a whole lot.''

Powers watched the moon rise and balance itself on the ridge, ready to float free. A single dead tree on the summit stood against it like a black-gloved hand held to a golden face.

Kellet said, "Just looka that ol' tree, so . . . strong-lookin' an' . . . so dead."

When the moon was adrift, Kellet said, "Fixed that door with a new beam an' good gudgeons. Man go to kick it down now'd have a job to do. She—"

Powers waited.

"—she never did use it. After she got well enough to get up an' around a bit, even. Just left it open. Mebbe she never thought about it. Mebbe she did, too. Nights, I'd stretch out in my bedroll, lay there, and wait. Pretty soon she'd call out, 'Good night, Kellet. Sleep good, now.' Thing like that, that's worth a passel o' farmin' an' carpenterin' . . .

"One night, ten-'leven days after I got there, woke up. She was cryin' there in the dark in t'other room. I called out what's the matter. She didn't say. Just kept a-bawlin'. Figgered mebbe her head hurt her. Got up, went to th' door. Asked her if she's all right. She just keeps a-cryin'—not loud, mind, but cryin' hard. Thing like that makes a man feel all tore up.

"Went on in. Called her name. She patted th' side o' th' bed. I set down. Put my hand on her face to see if she was gettin th' fever ag'in. Face was cool. Wet, too. She tuk my hand in her two an' held it hard up ag'in her mouth. I didn't know she was so strong.

"Set there quiet for two-three minutes. Got m' hand loose. Says, 'What you bawlin' for, ma'am?'

"She says, 'It's good to have you here.'

"I stood up, says, 'You git back to yore rest now, ma'am.' She—"

There were minutes between the words, but no change in his voice when he continued.

"—cried mebbe a hour. Stopped sudden, and altogether. Mebbe I slept after that, mebbe I didn't. Don't rightly recall.

"Next mornin' she's up bright an' early, fixin' chow. First time she's done it since she's hurt. Tole her, 'Whoa. Take it easy, ma'am. You don't want to tucker yoreself out.'

"She says, 'I coulda done this three days ago.' Sounded

mad. Don't rightly know who she's mad at. Fixed a powerful good breakfast.

"That day seemed the same, but it was 'way differ'nt. Other days we mostly didn't talk nothin' but business—caterpillars in th' tomato vines, fix a hole in th' smoke shed, an' like that. This day we talked th' same things. Difference was, we had to try hard to keep th' talk where it was. An' one more thing—didn't neither of us say one more word 'bout any work that might have to be done—tomorrow.

"Midday, I gathered up what was mine, an' packed my saddlebags. Brought my hoss up to th' shed an' watered him an' saddled him. Didn't see her much, but knowed she's watchin' me from inside th' house.

"All done, went to pat m'hoss once on the neck. Hit him so hard he shied. Right surprised m'self.

"She come out then. She stood a-lookin' at me. Says, 'Good-bye, Kellet. God bless you.'

"Says good-bye to her. Then didn't neither of us move for a minute. She says, 'You think I'm a bad woman.'

"Says, 'No sech a damn thing, ma'am! You was a sick one, an' powerful lonesome. You'll be all right now.'

"She says, 'I'm all right. I'll be all right long as I live,' she says, 'thanks to you, Kellet. Kellet,' she says, 'you had to think for both of us an' you did. Yo're a gentleman, Kellet,' she says.

"Mounted, then, an' rode off. On the rise, looked back, saw her still by th' shed, lookin' at me. Waved m'hat. Rode on."

The night was a white night now, since the moon had sucked its buoyant gold for its traveling silver. Powers heard Kellet turn over, and knew he could speak now if he cared to. Somewhere a mouse screamed briefly under an owl's silent talons. Distantly, a coyote's hungry call built itself into the echoing loneliness.

Powers said, "So that's what a gentleman is. A man that c'n think for two people when the time comes for it?"

"Naw-w," drawled Kellet scornfully. "That's just what she comes to believe because I never touched her."

Powers asked it, straight. "Why didn't you?"

A man will tell things, sometimes, things grown into him like the calluses from his wire cutters, things as much a part of him as, say, a notched ear or bullet scars in his belly, and his hearer should be a man who will not mention them after sun-up—perhaps not until his partner is dead—perhaps never.

Kellet said, "I cain't."

S. Omar Barker, in addition to being the premier maker of Old West rhymes, is an accomplished teller of stories. Among his many fine short stories is "Bad Company," a Western Writers of America Spur Award winner for Best Short Story of 1955; and the tale that follows, a memorable account of a bunch of trail-toughened Texas cowhands driving a herd of two thousand rebellious longhorns across Pudgamalodgy Creek.

Trail Fever

S. Omar Barker

Supper at the U Bar wagon that midsummer evening was by no means a-hurt with happiness, nor with cleanliness either. The only wahoo not mud-caked from boot heel to brisket was old Tuck Fargus, the cross-eyed cook.

"Dry me out an' you could lay me for a 'dobe," complained Midge Calley, heel-squatting where the glow of embers soon had his south end steaming.

"If dirt was a penny a pound," grunted Rusty Strayhorn, "I'd be worth a month's wages just for my scrapin's!"

"Which is more'n you'll ever add up to, clean!" Brazos Bill Endicott was eating left-handed tonight, thanks to an elbow painfully twisted in a futile struggle with a bogged steer, but his arid drawl sounded as breezy as usual. "Whichaway's Montana now, Cuff?"

Cuff Howell didn't answer. He and his nine-man crew of trail-toughened Texas cowhands had that day tried to push two thousand rebellious longhorns across a water called Pudgamalodgy Creek—and failed, at a cost of seventeen bog-buried steers.

There had been some cost in cowboy temper too. In six hundred hoof-beaten miles of dust and drought, good grass and bad, storms, stampedes and rivers to cross, these seventeen were the first U Bar cattle the prideful young trail boss had lost, and he was feeling a little stiff-necked about it. That could have been partly because he had tried the crossing despite the profane protests of red-haired Rusty Strayhorn that there wasn't a crossing within forty miles that would be safe for a mud turtle on stilts, much less a herd of steers. It was not the first time a little hair had been rubbed the wrong way between him and Rusty.

"Montana lays thataway!" Howell had gestured northward with a leather-cuffed arm. "We'll cross 'em!"

So they had tried. Almost all day they had tried, and no trail crew had ever tried harder. But tonight the U Bar herd, minus seventeen dead, was still south of the Pudgamalodgy, and Cuff Howell was in no pleasant temper.

They had hit the Cimarron and the Red in full flood and swum them both in true trail-driver style, but here was a different story. Mildly in flood from upcreek rains, still not more than a dozen feet of this sluggish little stream's sixty-foot width ran swimming water. The rest of its deceptive span was barely moving water no more than three to a dozen inches deep. But under that water lurked mud. Not quicksand. Mud. Mud without apparent bottom, tar-black when wet, turning a dull ash color as it caked dry on the legs of men, horses and the long-shanked Texas steers that balked and backed out of it in panic, in spite of all hell crowding hard behind them in the guise of whooping, rope-whapping cowboys.

Around midafternoon Cuff Howell's stubborn will had finally recognized reality and called it quits.

"I'll be a hog-tied horny toad!" he had sworn bitterly. "Six hundred miles behind us, and balked by a little crick that I could purt' near spit across! All right, boys, ream out your ears and let's see how many of these bogged beeves we can drag out before they drown!"

Around sundown, as they were dragging out the last still-living bog victims, an old speckled cow had come meandering through the cottonwoods on the opposite bank, paused to bawl a few times, then deliberately lunged into the muddy creek. She had floundered and struggled like a bug in a bowl of Pudgama-lodgy pudding, but still somehow made it across, thus adding insult to the indignity of the trail crew's failure. Clambering out on the south bank, the cow had trotted off to join the herd of steers now grazing a quarter of a mile away out on the flat, as if wallowing across mud-bound creeks were an everyday pastime.

"By the holy horny toads!" said Cuff Howell. "If that crazy critter can cross it, why can't my idiot steers?"

"The female of the species," said Brazos Bill, hunching his bull-like, slightly humped-over shoulders in the sort of half-clownish way he had, "gits more lonesome than the he! She heard the bawlin' an' come lookin' for company!"

Cuff Howell had then ridden along the bank, a slim ramrod in his muddy saddle, scowling at the route by which the cow had crossed.

"Tomorrow we'll cross this herd," he said, "or know the reason why!"

"One cow on her own ain't like two thousand steers pushed, Cuff," observed Brazos Bill. "If I was bossin' this beef, I'd hold up an' graze till she dries."

Ordinarily such a comment should have raised no hackles, but the young trail boss's judgment had that day been proved wrong, and Cuff Howell was a man who like to be right. There was a raw edge of touchy temper in his answer.

"It so happens you ain't bossin' this herd, cowboy!"

"Might not be a bad idea if he was," put in Rusty Strayhorn dryly. "Sometimes you git awful high an' mighty for the size of your diapers, Mister Howell!"

There were times in those rough days of rawhide riding men when a certain way of saying "mister" could touch off a ruckus. This might easily have been one of them if Brazos Bill hadn't picked that moment to pop Rusty Strayhorn behind the ear with a gob of mud. He followed it up by riding casually between the outspoken Rusty and their sore-minded trail boss.

"Cuff," he said, "let's go see if ol' Tuck's got the Java pot hot!"

So supper at the U Bar wagon that evening was something less than a joyous feast of fellowship; not the most propitious moment, perhaps, for a nester kid to come looking for his cow. Nobody noticed his approach. He simply materialized out of the shadows, a scrawny youngster, maybe around twelve years old, his old straw hat pushed back from a humorously pug-nosed face, his frazzled bib overalls rolled to the knees above mud-smeared bare feet and legs. He carried a cow halter and a short, frazzled rope over one arm, an ax on the other shoulder.

"Howdy," he said without noticeable timidity. "Who's the top tuckahoo of this sorry Texican outfit?"

"Now that," observed Brazos Bill, "could be a matter of opinion."

Cuff Howell ignored the dig. "Where the devil," he said, "did you come from?"

"Pap's homestead's over acrost the crick," the boy informed him. "I come after my cow that your ol' Texican cattle tolled off with their bawlin'. We had her about done weanin' her calf, so I reckon she got lonesome. Her name's Josephine."

"Yeah? What's yours?"

"*G-l-a-d*, Glad; *d-i-s*, dis. Gladdis! An' the first feller that laughs, I'll stomp him!"

For a couple of brief chuckles nobody got "stomped."

"Call me Gwendoline," said Brazos Bill. "How'd you manage to cross that crick without boggin'?"

"Rode over on a dang catfish!" The boy batted big blue eyes solemnly. "I'm fixin' to go ketch Josephine outa your herd, mister. You got any objections?"

He addressed himself to Brazos Bill, but it was Cuff Howell who answered. "You keep away from that herd, you savvy!" he warned sharply. "We got trouble enough without a stampede!"

"Then you better git Josephine outa there for me—or was you aimin' to steal her? Pap says a heap of Texicans ain't nothin' but cow thieves anyway!"

"You better mind your manners, Catfish," Brazos Bill warned him solemnly. "That's the ring-tailed ramrod himself you're talkin' to. He crumbles kids your size into his coffee! Ain't that right, Cuff?''

Cuff Howell seemed to be in no mood for cowboy joshing. "You go back and tell your pa I said we'll cut out his cow in due time, after we get the herd across,'' he told the kid shortly. "I got no time now to fool with strays.''

"You try drivin' Josephine acrost along with all them steers the way I seen you doin' today, an' you'll git her bogged down, sure as shootin'!'' The Catfish Kid stood right up in the front row and laid it on the taw line. "I come after my cow, Mister Texican, an' I ain't goin' back till I git her!''

"And just how,'' inquired Cuff Howell sarcastically, "do you figger you'd get her back across, even if you had her cut out of the herd?''

"Let her ride a catfish, same as I did. Me an' Josephine ain't from Texas. We're smart enough to cross a little ol' muddy crick!''

Without comment, Cuff Howell got up and went to refill his tin coffee cup.

"Catfish,'' said Brazos Bill, "don't you realize you're liable to get yourself tromped on, insultin' the great Lone Star State with that kind of talk?''

"If I was scared of Texicans,'' stated the Catfish Kid scornfully, "I'd quit chawin' an' learn to suck eggs!''

It was a ludicrous thing, even a comical thing, this business of a scrawny, ragged, barefooted nester's young'un putting on such a show of bravado and bold talk before a bunch of tough Texas trail men. Yet mere smart-aleck show-off it surely was not. "Biggity behavior''—yes, but with something about it too frank and open-faced to be seriously offensive; something even a little pitiful, as if here was a boy trying, however mistakenly, to act like a man because for some reason or other he felt he had to be one.

Even as the kid's untimid tongue boasted how unafraid of "Texicans'' he was, Brazos Bill saw his glance rest hungrily on the Dutch oven still half full of old Tuck's brown-crusted biscuits close beside the cook fire. Apparently the cross-eyed cooky saw it, too, but before either of them had time to act on a hospitable impulse, Cuff Howell spoke again.

"You got no business here, kid," he said brusquely, "but as long as you are, you just as well get you a plate and sample our beans."

"I'll bet they rattle in the plate," said the boy, but he got a tin plate, filled it and went to work on Texican chuck with considerable gusto.

"If you was that light in the gut," observed Brazos Bill, "no wonder you didn't bog down crossin' the crick!"

The Catfish Kid took time to relish a generous bite of sourdough biscuit, then grinned amiably.

"All I done," he announced, "was coon-trot an ol' cottonwood log acrost the deep part with a few armloads of brush I'd chopped, then kept throwin' it out ahead of me to step on till I got acrost the bog. The brush don't sink enough but what it holds you up till you hop onto the next one. That catfish ridin' was jest a joke."

"There you are, Mister Howell!" Rusty Strayhorn spread his red-knuckled hands. "Learn your longhorns to hop from brush to brush an' you've just as good as got 'em across!"

"You pick a poor time for smart-aleck talk, Rusty." The young trail boss spoke quietly, but by no means sweetly. "And while I think of it, I reckon you ain't forgot my callin' name."

Rusty set down his eating weapons and stood up. "I ain't forgot the tongue-whippin' you give me back at Doan's Crossing! Nor how long you've kept me eatin' dust on the drag. I've rode the trail with you as a plain cowhand, Mister Howell, an' by glory, if you don't start sweetenin' up purty soon, I'm liable to—"

"You're liable to swaller your cud, Rusty," broke in Brazos Bill, breezy as ever. "If anybody's goin' to whip a trail boss around here, it's gonna be me! Ain't that right, Cuff?"

Cuff Howell gave him a queer look. "Let me know when." He shrugged.

"Sick em!" said the Catfish Kid, and everybody but Cuff and Rusty laughed.

"You 'tend to your biscuit bitin', Catfish," warned Brazos Bill, "or you're liable to git your little tail stepped on!"

Still scowling, Rusty Strayhorn sat down again on his bedroll and began to make a smoke. The Catfish Kid sopped up the last of his gravy with a hunk of biscuit and began gathering up the U Bar crew's empty eating gear.

"You want these weapons washed," he asked the cook, "or shall I wipe 'em out on my shirttail?"

"You just leave 'em be," growled Tuck Fargus. "I don't want no mudcat messin' around my kitchen!"

"You go set on a stump an' scratch your itch, gran'pa," the boy advised him. "My ma learned me never to eat free without he'pin' the cook!"

It was some cause for surprise to the U Bar crew that the cranky old cook let him go ahead. Whether purposely or not, the song the kid picked to sing while he worked seemed singularly appropriate to the occasion:

> *"Oh, I come to a river an' I couldn't git across,*
> *Singin' polly-wolly-doodle all the day."*

"Boys," said Cuff Howell, abruptly breaking a considerable spell of silence, "tomorrow we're goin' to build us a bridge across this creek!"

"In a pig's eye!" said Rusty Strayhorn.

Cuff ignored him. "If a little brush throwed in the mud held up this kid, a lot of brush will hold up logs. There's plenty of cottonwoods within draggin' distance and we've got three axes, countin' this youngster's. How many of you boys ever done any ax work?"

"I chopped off an ol' rooster's head once for a preacher's daughter down in Deaf Smith County," said Brazos Bill. "She was a yaller-haired filly, sorter Percheron built an'—"

"I hired out to drive cattle," broke in Rusty, "not to swing an ax!"

"You'll get used to it," said the trail boss dryly. "I want to get this crossin' made. The Three Bar herd ain't over two days behind us."

"So what?"

"I still aim to get to Montana ahead of them. You know the U Bars ain't contracted. It'll be first come, best sold. Tomorrow we'll build a bridge."

* * *

Bridging Pudgamalodgy Creek turned out to be no simple task. Well before sunup, cowboy arms far more accustomed to swinging a rope were swinging axes, felling cottonwoods, lopping off the branches and chopping the trunks into logs about fifteen feet long. Other cowboys dragged the lopped brush to the bridge site by rope and saddle horn. Even old Tuck Fargus was pressed into service to snake logs with the chuck-wagon team.

Cuff Howell bossed the job of piling brush in the muck to serve as a foundation for the logs to rest on, but he didn't spare his own sweat either.

Neither did the Catfish Kid, though a good deal of his energy seemed to be used up in trotting back and forth from one part of the job to another, alternately giving unsought advice, getting in the way and demanding the immediate return of his cow.

"You ox-wallopers chop like a one-eyed ol' woman whippin' a carpet," he commented. "Them stumps look like they'd been gnawed off by a sore-toothed beaver!"

"You go learn your gran'ma to milk ducks." Brazos Bill grinned, and went on chopping.

But Rusty Strayhorn handed the kid his ax. "Maybe you'd like to show us how it's done, blabber-mouth!"

The Catfish Kid took the ax and spit on his hands. "Cheewah!" he grunted, and swung it.

His scrawny arms lacked power to sink the bit very deep, but in half a dozen swings he trued up Rusty's messy notch.

"Pap learnt me axin' before he taken the lung fever back in Kentucky," he informed them, handing Rusty back his ax. "I got to go see that ol' Cuff ain't pilin' that brush with the ends all one way!"

"You'd think it was his bridge," said Midge Calley as the kid trotted off.

"Why not?" Brazos Bill shrugged. "It was his brush-hoppin' that give Cuff the idea."

"A heck of an idea!" grunted Rusty. "If there's two things I hate, it's a stiff-necked trail boss an' a smart-aleck brat!" He threw down his ax, ruefully rubbing a blister puffing up in one palm. "I'm quittin'!"

"Little red bull, when his tail got sore,
Said he wasn't gonna switch flies no more!"

It was a little song Brazos Bill had made up to try to cheer up the Slash O camp one night after a perilous crossing of the flooded Red nearly two years ago, a crossing during which Brazos Bill had nearly drowned saving two other cowboys who had got knocked off their horses by floating logs. Remembering the occasion, Rusty gave him a queer look.

"Brazos," he said, "Cuff was a purty good feller as a plain cowhand. What's come over him to make him such a rannicky trail boss?"

"He's young." The big cowboy shrugged. "An' two thousand steers is a heap of another man's proputty to be responsible for. I reckon it sobers a man some."

"It don't have to sour him! He can't even grin anymore! I'm gittin' to where I hate the son of a gun's guts!"

"An' I wouldn't blame him for hatin' yours, the way you been giggin' him ever since Doan's Crossing."

"You heard the tongue-whippin' he gave me for takin' them few drinks at ol' Doan's Store!"

"You mean for goin' on night guard half drunk." Brazos grinned. "Suppose you'd of belched an' started a stampede?"

"That ain't no reason to keep me ridin' the drag. I'm as good a man on point or swing as ever went up the trail! An' now blisterin' my hands on an ax handle. By glory, Brazos, I'm quittin'!"

"You got trail fever, sorehead!" Brazos Bill grinned. "Let's you an' me go see if Cuff wants to shift you to the draggin' job awhile."

"To heck with you!" growled Rusty, but he went. It is not always easy to refuse a man who has once saved your life.

Up at the bridge site Cuff Howell was dragging the Catfish Kid out of a pothole into which he had tumbled while trying, against orders, to re-lay some brush the way he thought it ought to be.

"Now you get away from here—and stay away!" Cuff had the kid by the shirt collar, apparently fixing to kick his pants, when Brazos Bill laid a hand on his arm.

"Cuff," he said with that queer, half-clownish hunch of his big shoulders, "I got a man here that ain't worth hog scrapin's with an ax. Whyn't you put him to snakin' brush awhile?"

Howell turned the kid loose. It would have been hard to say whether he looked a little ashamed or only tight-lipped from raw-edged nerves.

"Brazos," he said, as if it were an effort to speak quietly, "some of these days you're goin' to use up your credit. All I'm tryin' to do is build a bridge. I don't give a hang who works at what, as long as it keeps the job movin'!"

It would have been a good time for Rusty to keep his mouth shut, but he didn't.

"Mister Howell," he inquired sweetly, "did you ever try pushin' a herd of longhorns onto a fresh-built bridge?"

"I can't say that I have, but—"

"Then you're due to learn somethin'. I'll bet you anything you say that you cain't make 'em cross it!"

"My good Christian friend," said the trail boss, with a challenging gleam in his eye, "if I don't cross the U Bars on this bridge, you'll draw my wages when we get to Montana! If I do cross 'em, you'll stop bellyachin' for the rest of this trip!"

"You've bought you a bet." Rusty shrugged. "What can I lose?"

"Your job if you don't get to work!" snapped Cuff. "I want this bridge done in time for crossin' tomorrow."

The Catfish Kid had not sidled away very far. "You're pilin' them branches crooked agin," he advised with a tentative grin. "Can't I ever learn you Texicans nothin'?"

Piled crooked or not, once there was enough of it, the cottowood brush ceased to sink, furnishing an adequate though none-too-steady foundation upon which sweating cowhands grunt-wrestled log after log into place, crowding them close together, plugging cracks full of twig brush, and finally covering the whole works with load after back-busting load of ax-cut sod carried on old scraps of wagon sheet.

What with the difficulty of dropping stringers across the dozen feet of deepwater channel and the time it took to throw up brush wings to funnel an approach to the bridge, it was already dusk on the evening of the second day by the time Cuff Howell took a final walk across the crude, somewhat quivery structure and called it a bridge.

"There she lays, boys," Cuff spoke with some pride. "Dry crossin' for the U Bar herd!"

"In a pig's eye!" said Rusty.

"Purty fair job—for a bunch of Texicans," breezed the Catfish Kid. "I wish some of you ox-wallopers would rustle Josephine outa that herd, so I could git home with her."

"Holy horny toads!" snorted the trail boss. "Don't you never give up?"

It would have been another good time for Rusty to keep his mouth shut.

"Come on, kid," he offered, knowing the trail boss would veto it. "I'll cut that cow for you right now."

Cuff Howell could have said, "Better not, Rusty. I'd rather leave the herd as quiet as possible till we get this crossing made." Instead he said, "You won't do any such of a darn-fool thing, cowboy!"

Even as an order, which it was his right to give, he could have spoken less sharply. But there it was again: two good trail men with their neck hair up, touch and go for trouble, for no good reason, as far as Brazos Bill could see, except that once started, friction fed on friction, building up into a kind of trail fever Brazo's Bill had more than once seen wind up in a shooting.

"Cuff," said Brazos, "durned if I don't wonder sometimes if it might not have been smarter to let both of you ring-tails drown! We've got our bridge built. Let's go to the wagon. I'm as hungry as an ol' she-wolf with sixteen pups!"

Rusty shrugged. Cuff reached for his horse. Neither one said anything more.

That night, with Brazos Bill and Rusty on fourth guard and dawn not far away, the U Bar herd stampeded. By thin moonlight Brazos saw what had spooked them: the Catfish Kid, prowling on foot, probably in search of his cow. It was not a bad run, as stampedes go, but it took till midmorning to get the herd regathered and quieted down enough to try the new bridge. Brazos saw that the boy's speckled cow was still in the herd, but the Catfish Kid seemed to have disappeared. Unless necessary to keep Cuff from blaming Rusty for the stampede, Brazos had meant to hold his tongue about what had caused it. Cuff saved him the trouble.

"I'd like to get my hands on that nester brat!" the trail boss said. "I'd learn him to go prowlin' around a herd when he's been told not to!"

"I seen him steppin' long and foggin' for home," said Tuck Fargus. "I reckon the poor kid savvied you'd be on his tail if you caught him."

"Poor kid, hell!" growled Cuff. "All right, let's cross these cattle!"

Experienced cowhands under the orders of a trail boss with cow savvy, the U Bar crew strung the longhorns out, trail style, in a line nearly a mile long and pointed them quietly toward the bridge. A big line-back steer stepped out briskly in the lead, as he had done all the way from Texas. It looked easy.

Fifty yards from the bridge the line-back threw up his head and stopped. So did the dozen secondary leaders close behind him. Quietly, Rusty and three other cowboys eased up from farther back. Cuff rode slowly on ahead. Sometimes cattle will follow a man on horseback. Moving their horses slow and easy, Brazos and Rusty crowded them a little. Heads high, eying the strange structure suspiciously, the leaders moved forward. Slowly Cuff rode onto the bridge. It quivered a little. The big line-back stopped again, snuffing at the freshly placed sod. He hesitated a second, then stepped gingerly onto the bridge, two more steers close behind him. The unsteadiness under their tread was no more than a faint quiver, but it was enough. With a windy snort, they whirled and lunged back off the bridge.

Head high, weaving a little in search of an opening, the line-back leader headed back for what he considered safer territory. Rusty could easily have let him pass, but he didn't. With swift cow-pony zigzags he blocked the steer's flight and turned him. Brazos turned two that came his way, the other cowboys several more.

But it was no use. When a dozen, two dozen, three dozen steers suddenly decided to get out of there, three dozen cowboys could not have held them. All they could do was swing back to mill the herd to keep it from stampeding.

Cuff Howell came riding back from the bridge. "Soon as they settle," he said quietly, "we'll try it again."

Try it again they did, again and many agains. They tried easing them, crowding them, rushing them. They tried driving the remuda across ahead of them in the vain hope of forcing them to follow. They brought the whole herd around in a circle a mile wide, let the usual leaders pass the bridge, then cut off fifty or so of the less alert loiterers that made up the drag and tried to crowd them across. But these also had promised their mammas never to set foot on a fresh-built log bridge.

They tried a flying wedge of a mere dozen steers with all hands whooping at their heels, in the hope that once a few had crossed, the smell of their passing or the sight of them on the far bank would serve to lull longhorn fears. They got ten of these well onto the bridge, but when a sudden balk crowded three off into the mire, they had to give that up too.

At sunset the U Bar crew was a sweat-drained, nerve-frazzled baffled bunch of buckaroos, and not a single U Bar steer had yet crossed Cuff Howell's wonderful bridge.

"Now if—that—don't beat—hell!" By now Cuff had given up the "holy horny toads" and switched to straight swearing. "Rusty, it begins to look like you win your damn bet!"

Rusty went on rolling a smoke and said nothing.

Off to the south a thin dust hazed the air.

"That'll be the Three Bars," said Cuff. "If their steers will cross it, we can't refuse 'em the lead. Maybe ours will follow."

It was, in effect, an admission of defeat.

"Look yonder!" said Rusty suddenly.

Watching the distant dust, they had not noticed the Catfish Kid's approach. Now he came on across the bridge, half leading, half driving a nine-months-old speckled calf.

"Honest, Mister Texican," he addressed the trail boss in a tone of grave anxiety, "I sure never meant to booger your herd last night. If you want to kick my pants, I'll stand for it without hitchin'—only don't kick too durn hard!"

"Forget it," said Cuff shortly. "Brazos, a couple of you boys just as well cut out this kid's cow and let him have her. Maybe he can get her across the bridge, anyhow!"

"Say, by golly!" Brazos Bill grinned suddenly. "Supposin'—"

"What I was figgerin'," broke in the Catfish Kid, "Jasper ain't been weaned so long but what Josephine'll reconnize him. If one of you tuckahoos'll git a rope on him an' yank him along purty fast, he'll git to bawlin', an' Josephine'll foller him, an' she'll git to bawlin', an' when them Texican steers hear 'em, some of them'll come arunnin', an' they'll git to bawlin', an'—"

"Locate the kid's cow," broke in Cuff Howell. "Shape up the herd, string out a hundred or so of the drag to follow her, and—"

But already he was talking to hoof-dusty air. Well knowing that nothing but the smell of blood could excite range cattle like the distressed bellering of a calf, especially with its mother adding her long-tongued vocal anxiety to the din, the U Bar cowboys were already on their way with no need for further orders.

It was Rusty Strayhorn's rope that dragged poor bellering Jasper through a fringe of the herd, out again with Josephine bawling behind him, then onto the bridge and across it, a string-out of excited steers crowding snuffily at her heels, too stirred up even to notice whether they were on a quivering bridge or the good solid earth. Quickly the strange excitement spread through the herd, until it was all the U Bar crew could do to pinch the crowding cattle down to a line thin enough for the narrow bridge to hold.

Less than an hour later, close behind the last steer across, Brazos Bill let out a wild cowboy yell of triumph, in which even a stiff-necked trail boss and a nester's brat spraddled behind the big cowboy's saddle raucously joined.

Half a mile northward the herd leaders were already spreading out to graze, their excitement all but forgotten. Some distance off to the left, Rusty and Midge were holding the Catfish Kid's now quieted cow and calf out of the herd for him. Giving the drags a parting shove, Brazos Bill rode over there. So did Cuff Howell, still straight, but no longer like a starched ramrod in the saddle.

"Well, Cuff," Rusty said, grinning, omitting the mock respect of "mister" for the first time in weeks, "it looks like you win a bet!"

For almost the first time since Doan's Crossing, Cuff Howell's face lost its thin-lipped look in a wide grin.

"I never noticed you sparin' any sweat to keep me from it," he said. "I can make out with a man that don't never forget he's a cowboy."

It was, in the way of the hired men on horseback of that fargone day, a verbal handshake. It meant, among other things, that tomorrow Rusty Strayhorn would no longer be riding the drag.

The Catfish Kid slid down from behind Brazos Bill's saddle, rubbing his sweaty crotch.

"Well, Josephine," he addressed the speckled cow, "maybe that'll learn you not to run off visitin' with a bunch of longhorns!" He grinned up at the circle of cowboys and began putting his frazzled halter on the now subdued cow.

"Catfish," said Brazos Bill, "we ain't sure which one we ought to kiss, you, the calf or the cow!"

"Don't let him hurraw you, Catfish!" Cuff Howell got off his horse to help the boy halter his cow. "The fact is we're mightly obliged to all three of you. A couple of the boys will help take your cattle home, but meantime—"

"Don't need no help, Mister Texican!"

"I can believe that," Cuff broke in dryly. "But we might, if we hit any more boggy creeks between here and Montana. I'd like mighty well to rustle a horse, saddle and wages for a cook's helper learnin' to be a cowboy—if you want to go along."

The boy's shrug was elaborately scornful, his tone brash and breezy, his grin wide, but there was a wistful look in his big blue eyes that not a cowboy present could miss.

"Thanks for the free biscuits," he answered, "but not countin' pap's claim to look after, I'd as soon take up with the coyotes as a bunch of Texican ox-wallopers!"

Looking back as they rode on to catch up with the U Bar herd, Brazos Bill saw that the Catfish Kid stood a long time watching them go, and once he waved his old straw hat. Four cowboy sombreros waved in answer.

"Barrin' a sick pap"—Brazos Bill hunched his big shoulders and chuckled—"he'd have made us a curly wolf, Cuff. I wonder what kind of a fit he'll throw when he finds that ten-dollar gold piece you slipped in his overalls while helpin' him halter ol' Josephine!"

A. B. Guthrie's The Big Sky *has been hailed by readers and critics alike as one of the finest Western historical novels ever penned; his other meticulously researched novels such as* The Way West, These Thousand Hills, *and* Arfive *have also received high acclaim. In addition to these, he has written a successful series of mystery novels (*Wild Pitch, The Genuine Article*) and several short pieces of fiction and nonfiction. Wry and amusing, "The Therefore Hog" is ample evidence of his prowess in the short-story form.*

The Therefore Hog

A. B. Guthrie, Jr.

Just once did I get the best of a bed hog, and that was in Ogalally, Nebraska, in 1881 or thereabouts.

He was a ranch cook name of House—Slaughter House we called him, of course. The main thing about him, outside of being cantankery like all cooks, was that his eyes was so weak he couldn't tell bacon from beans without his specs on. The specs was as thick as one of his flapjacks, which a man had to sit straight to look over. His mind wasn't that deep, but he thought it was, specially after he had read a book or sucked a bottle. Both of them items was failings of his. He always said he would roam the whole range of writing except his eyes hobbled him. On a bender he was what you might call a hard keeper.

After beef roundup one season me and him decided we ought to put some money in circulation, so we asked for our time and lit out.

Winter came early that year, early and hard, and by and by,

95

with a blizzard blowing that made a man hanker for hell, we found we was there in Ogalally, having drunk our way yonder over trails that was blank now in our minds, specially his. Both of us, specially him again, was saddle-sore from riding saloon and, to heal up on, needed nothing so much as a pillow. Trouble was, people had bunched up in the storm, and there wasn't but one hotel room empty and it with what you'd have to tally as a runt or honeymoon bed.

Now as a bedmate a colicky bronc couldn't hold a candle to Slaughter, which I knew from before. He would jump and wrastle and thrash and heave himself from rail to rail, putting into the act for good measure a fearsome lot of whistles and groans and death strangles. About the time you would think, thank God, he had give up the ghost, he would catch a tail hold on his dying breath and go to bucking and snorting again.

"Slaughter," I said, looking at the honeymoon bed, "who gets the bunk?"

Slaughter's eyes was red and blue lakes that looked like they might flood over the bank of his glasses. Booze made him speak slow but impressive. He answered, "Both of us, naturally. How much range you want?"

"Anyone ranges with you gets the tallow run off of him," I told him.

"You're becomin' damn particular," he said and drawed on his book learning. "Look! I'm willing to sleep with you, not as it's a treat. You're not willing to sleep with me. Therefore I get the bed."

"Therefore!" I came back at him. "Where you get therefore?"

"You got an ignorant mind," he said, standing not too steady. "Therefore therefore. What follers follers. That's how come therefore."

I let the therefores have it, being too frail to fuss much, but it galled me, I tell you.

We went downstairs, where Slaughter said he'd have a little hair of the dog and wound up with most of the pelt. He was a hard keeper all right. Then we ate a bait and picked up my bedroll at the livery stable and came back to the room. I spread the roll out on the floor. Slaughter took off his coat and boots and pants and hat and climbed into his nice soft bed, letting out a sigh as it gave to his bones.

There was a little old stove in the room, which we had stoked up before we went out. Like all stoves in them days, saving the old kitchen range, it was mighty unreasonable, being either ice-cold or red-hot and no in-between. Right now it was showing the devil how fires ought to burn.

You know how it is when an outdoor man goes to town. He can't bear the heat like city people. Too used to bedding down outside with his back for a tick and his belly for a blanket. Sweats in his clothes and fights off the soogans. So, cold as the weather was, I raised the window some. I hung my cartridge belt on a chair that happened to stand right at the window. In them days I cased my gun in an open-toed holster, thinking it made me look dangerouser.

Seeing me hang up my rigging reminded Slaughter he hadn't took off his glasses. He put them on a little table close to his hand, telling me he usually had to get up at night and wouldn't know where to begin unless he had them on.

What with his blood running anyhow fifty-proof, he went to sleep right away and right away started his exercises. From where I was I could see the sky had cleared. There was just the cold now and the wind, blowing a little spray of snow through the open window. By and by, in an hour or so, up sailed the moon, bright as a dollar. It showed my gun with the frost silvered on the muzzle of it. It showed Slaughter's big foot, too, which he had poked from the soogans. It was then my bright idea begun to glimmer.

I hunched out of my bedroll and took Slaughter's specs off the table and laid them by the baseboard. Then I slipped my six-shooter out of its case and drew that frosty muzzle along the palm of his foot.

Slaughter reared up in bed, and maybe you've heard a bear bawl. He grabbed for his foot, which he found, and then for his specs, which he didn't.

"Mike!" he yelled at me. "Mike!"

I let him yell some more before I said, "Whassa matter?" like I was just coming out of sleep. While he was making all that ruckus, I had crawled back to my bed.

"Somep'n burned me," he said. "On the foot. Where's my specs?"

I asked, "Somep'n burned you?"

"Like a brand," he said.

"Slaughter," I told him like I was a doctor, "you ain't at yourself"—which I don't need to add he wasn't.

"Where's them specs?" he wanted to know while he pawed the table to find them. He left off the pawing to feel again of his foot. His voice came out kind of hushed as his fingers found the wet streak that was melted frost. "It left a track."

"Slaughter, old boy," I said, still acting the doctor, "I was afraid of this."

He asked, "What?"

"Whiskey," I said. "It's done caught up with you."

He called me a fool and some other things, ending up with, "Think I dunno when I'm hurt?"

"People see snakes," I told him. "Purple and pink and all colors. No use to tell them there's no snakes around."

"Imagination don't leave no track," he said. "Get me them specs! Light the lamp!"

I made out to feel for the specs, though what I was doing was putting my six-gun back there by the window so's I'd be in business again. "They're not here," I announced.

"I put 'em there," he answered. "I know I put 'em there."

"That nose paint," I said. "You got to get off of it, Slaughter, old pardner. Promise me you won't take none for a spell. Your foot still hurting?"

He said, "Not so much"—like he didn't want to admit it—"but don't think it didn't."

"Sure. Sure," I answered in a good bedside way. "Now go back to sleep. Just go to sleep. We'll find your specs in the morning."

He grumbled around some more but pretty soon went to thrashing and strangling again, getting what he called a good night's rest.

It took him longer on the second go-round to bust out of the covers, but when he did he done it better. It wasn't just the foot alone that came out but a fair section of the tail. Part of it was where the saddle had wore a hole in his drawers. There he was, him and his bare anatomy, and there was my six-gun, replated with frost.

What went on before wasn't nothing to now. This time, from a lying start, he sailed out of bed like a trout and flapped on the floor, yelling like the head chief of the Sioux.

I listened awhile and then said, acting half asleep and half sore, "Now what's the matter?"

"It come again," he answered. From his voice you would have thought I was deaf.

"On the foot?" I asked.

"It moved up," he said. Him talking so delicate showed how upset he was. "But it's the same thing. It left a track."

"Slaughter," I said, "you poor feller."

He went to begging. "Find my glasses, Mike. Please find my glasses."

"Why, they're right here," I told him, picking them up and at the same time putting my gun back. "Don't you even recollect laying them here? On this teensy table?"

"There!" he said, real indignant. "You couldn't find 'em your own self a while back!"

"I didn't look for them," I answered, walking over and putting them in his hand, for he had got to his feet. "You never asked me."

He hooked the specs over his ears and looked at me there in the moonlight. He shook his head so solemn that he had to catch a step to keep balanced. "Someone's sure got the shakes," he said.

"You'll be all right," I told him. "Get back to bed. Lie down. Probably you'll feel better by morning, though it usually takes three or four days. I'll bring you plenty of soup."

He sized me up again, his eyes swimming with moonlight and whiskey and questions, and then without a word he put on his hat and began pulling on his pants.

I said, "Where do you think you're going?"

"Any place," he said, not speaking to me so much as to himself. "Any place at all just to get shed of things."

I asked him what things.

He finished dressing and went to the door. Dignified is the word for the way he walked, the more so because he tried so stiff to keep from weaving. With his hand on the knob he turned round and spoke very preacherlike. "To get shed of fools," he said, "damn fools and them fire snails." Then he went out, closing the door firm behind him.

And therefore I climbed into that nice empty bed.

This compelling and top-notch depiction of the struggle between a cowboy, Travis, and a wild roan mustang is an example of H. S. De Rosso's considerable talent with offbeat Western themes. De Rosso produced hundreds of yarns for the pulps (and occasionally for slick magazines) in the 1940s and 1950s, as well as such excellent novels as .44, The Man from Texas, and End of the Gun.

Fear in the Saddle

H. S. DeRosso

Travis awoke and lay awhile, listening to the sounds coming from the corral. In his mind's eye he could see the restless pacing of the roan. It seemed that the animal was never still. In one way this might be a good thing, for this constant fitfulness could tire the animal, thus making the job ahead a trifle easier. But just thinking about it turned Travis cold at the pit of his stomach.

Travis rose and dressed. He cursed a little, quietly and disgustedly, while he cooked his breakfast. He wondered if he could get anything down. He kept thinking about what he had to do this morning.

Down in the corral the roan still paced.

Though there was no taste to it, Travis forced some food into himself. Then he built a cigarette and sat with his legs stretched out to savor an after-breakfast smoke. He told himself there was nothing better than a cigarette after eating, but he knew the real reason was that it helped prolong the time before he went to the roan.

Finally, he rose to his feet, full of disgust with himself. After all, this wasn't the first time he'd tried to break a horse! He'd been doing this for ten of his twenty-five years. This was his livelihood. He'd ridden the buckers in Calgary, Pendleton, Cheyenne. He was one of the best riders in the business. He'd topped tougher broncs than this wild roan that he'd captured a month ago. But all that lay in the past, he realized sickeningly. This was something different.

He decided it was no good standing here, thinking about it. The thoughts only tormented him. The thing to do was to get it over with.

The roan heard Travis coming and abruptly stopped its pacing. It turned to face Travis, ears cocked, tense and waiting. The roan snorted once, then was quiet, watching Travis crossing to the corral.

Travis stopped and stared through the bars and as he looked he thought he felt a pain in his right thigh where his leg had been broken. But that had happened over a year ago and more than one doctor had pronounced the leg healed. Still, the pain persisted as Travis stood there. He knew it was only in his mind but it felt real enough. Travis began to sweat.

Travis clenched his teeth and stepped into the corral. The roan snorted and paced nervously to the far end of the enclosure.

Travis shook out a loop in his rope. He didn't have too much trouble with the roan. By now the animal had grown accustomed to being roped and snubbed and saddled. Travis had been patient with the horse. He had taught it first to become used to a halter, then to a blanket on its back, then the saddle, and finally weights on the saddle.

Now it was time to ride the roan. Travis felt weak and sick.

The horse was snubbed tight to a post which Travis had sunk into the ground at one end of the corral. It stood docilely enough, tension apparent only in the way it flicked back its ears.

Travis stood undecided. He told himself he couldn't be too careful. This abandoned ranch he had selected for his job was in an isolated part of these mountains. No one ever passed by here. A man could not be too careful with a wild horse when he was by himself. But Travis had to be alone. The shame was so great in him that he could not endure the thought of displaying his cowardice to another.

Travis began to feel that he should try a weight on the roan again today. Perhaps the horse wasn't ready to be ridden yet. He had to be careful about that because he was alone, Travis thought, and then he flushed with disgust and mortification. He knew this was just another excuse to put off riding the roan.

Travis could feel the muscles of his thighs quivering as he quietly loosened the rope holding the roan snubbed. For a wild instant he hoped the roan would jerk away from him so that he couldn't mount but the animal stood quietly, not flicking a muscle.

Travis sucked in his breath and then he was going up into the saddle. The roan reacted swiftly. Even before Travis touched the seat of the kak the animal was going up in the air, its back arching. Travis's boots found the stirrups quickly.

The roan kept its back arched and began crow-hopping across the corral. This maneuver would never have been enough to unseat Travis in the past. But he envisioned himself being hurtled through the air and then striking the ground and the roan bearing down on him, fore hoofs rising, flailing, to come crashing down on him as he cowered helplessly on the ground.

He was alone, his mind shrieked at him. He had to unload of his own will. He had to pile off of his own choosing if he didn't want to be trampled again. There was no one around to drive off the roan and drag him away as there had been in Calgary. Panic filled Travis's throat.

He hit the ground on both feet and the momentum of it carried him forward and down, but he spread his hands before him and saved himself from going flat on his face.

You've got to get out of here, his mind screamed at him. *You've got to run before he tramples you.*

Then he was on his feet and streaking for the corral bars. Terror shrieked in his brain. He went through the bars so fast that he sprawled on the ground, his cheek scraping the dirt. For a moment he lay there, breathing hard, quivering, and sick with fear, afraid to rise and afraid almost to hope that he was safe.

But the worst of the panic soon passed and Travis rolled over and sat up.

He stared at the corral and saw the roan on the far side, watching him. It came then to Travis that the horse had made no effort to trample him. The instant he had quit the saddle the roan must have stopped bucking. The horse wasn't even breathing hard. It stood there with ears cocked forward, looking at Travis as if it understood what had gone on in the man's mind.

Travis put his face in his hands and shuddered. He could have wept with helplessness.

He lay on his bunk, blowing cigarette smoke up at the ceiling. The quivering of his insides had stopped and fear seemed a distant and alien thing to him now. He supposed it was because he had knocked off for the rest of the day and wouldn't have to face the job until the next morning.

He told himself there was no compulsion about this thing except what he himself wanted to do. It wasn't necessary for him to follow the rodeo circuit to earn his keep. He could do all right in some other line of business. It wasn't even a question of being unable to ride a horse. The broken ones he could ride without a qualm. It was the buckers that turned him hollow and quivering inside, but he didn't have to stick to bronc-riding for a living.

I guess I'll quit, he thought, puffing slowly on his smoke. *It wouldn't be too hard to give a reason. I can say I'm all busted up inside and the docs have told me never to top a bronc again.*

But he felt ill and miserable at the thought. Whatever he might tell others, he himself would know he had quit because he was afraid. He was yellow.

Travis turned his face to the wall and cursed with a studied, frustrated vehemence. *Yellow,* his mind kept whispering. He just didn't have any guts anymore.

Travis awoke before dawn. He lay awhile in his bunk, listening for sounds from the corral, but they didn't begin until the break of day. Then, because he couldn't stand hearing them and because he wanted to get an early start, Travis jumped out of bed.

After breakfast, he went outside. The morning was clear and cool. There was a stiff breeze coming down from the mountain, stirring the tops of the pines and cedars, and raising occasional small swirls of dust in the corral.

The roan was staring almost wistfully out through the bars, at the timbered slopes and pitches. It seemed immersed in this study and paid no attention to Travis as he came down from the house.

Travis stopped and watched the roan awhile. The horse still did not face Travis although it must have heard the jingle of his spurs as he had come up. It just went on staring, with a longing that was apparent to the man.

Travis found himself thinking, *It's a shame to coop him up like this. He never hurt anybody. He wants to be out there, free and wild. He should be turned loose. . . .*

Then the feeling came to Travis that this was just the old excuse taking another turn. It was the cowardice working in him.

Angry with himself, he stepped into the corral. He roped the roan and snubbed it to the post. The horse was quite difficult this morning and there was a fine film of sweat on Travis's face by the time he got the animal tied to the post. The roan wouldn't stand still. It knocked the saddle off three times before Travis got it cinched on.

"I don't like this any more than you do," he growled at the horse, "but it's something that has to be done. If you'd just go along with me, we'd get it over with that much faster. Now stand still, or I'll take a whip to you."

The instant that Travis released the snub the roan jerked away. Travis grabbed for the lines, but the roan moved so fast and hard that the reins were ripped out of Travis's grip. Snorting, the roan whirled and raced to the other end of the corral.

Cursing savagely, Travis went after the roan, but before he was within ten feet of the animal, it broke wildly past him, spraying him with grit and dust kicked up by its pounding hoofs.

Travis got his rope. He shook out a loop and advanced on the roan. For an instant the horse bared its teeth and its ears flattened against its head. The roan emitted a shrill, angry snort and broke.

The horse seemed to hurtle straight at Travis and he had a swift, terrifying vision of going down under those churning hoofs, but at the last instant the roan swerved, and as it pounded past him, Travis dropped the loop over its neck. The roan fought all the way back to the snubbing-post but Travis finally got it tied again.

Travis was breathing hard. The roan kept shying and snorting and Travis saw it was no use trying to do anything with the horse until it had calmed down.

He was angry again, at himself and at the horse. If things had not gone wrong, he might have had the ordeal over with by this time, he might have had the roan broken by now. Instead, he still had to start and as he waited, watching the roan, he could feel the first tentative flutters of fear in his thighs and in his belly. He knew that in a little while he was going to feel sick again and he almost wept with anger.

He edged in on the roan and caught the halter and began patting the horse's neck. "I'm not going to hurt you, boy," he told the roan. "It's just something that's got to be done. I've just got to top you. For myself. Can't you see? Damn it, why do you keep fighting me?"

The roan quieted. The wicked, perverse glint seemed to go out of its eyes. Now it stood there almost still.

"We're going to get along all right together. I know we are," Travis said, with an assurance he didn't feel. He kept stroking the roan's neck.

The roan was very still now. It seemed relaxed and no longer vigilant. Continuing to stroke it with his right hand, Travis released the snap with his left, and before the roan realized that once more it was free, Travis had vaulted up into the saddle.

The roan whirled around twice as it pulled away from the post. Travis had both feet in the stirrups and this time he had a good seat and for a moment he was almost overwhelmed with confidence.

Travis could feel his body sway with the old ease and effortlessness with the first harsh movements of the roan and he almost sang with joy. The roan kicked up its hind end and then reared sharply. Then it started whirling again, raising a great cloud of dust that almost gagged Travis, but he went along with it, sticking like a burr to the saddle, exulting all the while.

Abruptly the roan changed tactics. Its back arched and it began hopping, stiff-legged, across the corral. With each try the horse seemed to go higher and come down harder. The jolts began to jar up Travis's spine. He felt the joy, the assurance, ebb from him.

It was not a question of sticking in the saddle anymore, he thought. He was sure he could do that but there was something wrong inside him. His belly was filled with pain. It was as if the jolts had torn something loose in there and it kept bouncing up and down, agonizingly, with each movement of the roan.

The doctors had lied. He wasn't cured at all. He was all torn up and busted inside. He could feel something break loose and rise up to gag in his throat. He couldn't breathe. He was a sick man; he had no business on a bucking horse.

The roan had reached the other end of the corral and now it swerved up against the poles, trying to scrape Travis off the saddle. Travis saw the bars come at him and he waited for no more.

He threw himself wildly out of the kak. He hit the ground badly and went sprawling. But he recovered quickly, was halfway to his feet when the roan hit him.

It was so sudden and unexpected that at first Travis had no idea he had been struck. He felt himself being barreled along over the ground and only then it occurred to him that the roan had turned on him.

Panic clogged Travis's throat. Luckily, he had been knocked toward the side of the corral, and as the roan, squealing with rage, came smashing back, Travis rolled to safety beneath the bottom bar.

He lurched up on his knees, trembling with fear and fury. His face was wet, but he didn't know if it was from sweat or tears or blood. His thigh ached furiously and for a moment he was afraid that his leg had been broken again.

The roan smashed up against the side of the corral once more. Then the horse put its head down between its front legs and went bucking frenziedly around the enclosure. Travis shook his fist at the roan.

"I'll fix you," he shouted. "I'll show you if you can get away with this!"

He jumped to his feet, raging with defeat and frustration, and ran up to the house. He got his Winchester and ran back to the corral.

"Damn you," he screamed at the roan, "see how you like this!"

He had the sights lined up with the roan's head when a sudden thought struck Travis and he froze.

He was all right inside. There was nothing wrong with his belly, there was nothing loose in him, there was nothing clogging his throat anymore. It had been panic that had caused the pain and had thrown him off the roan.

You're really yellow, Travis, an inner voice said to him.

"I'm not yellow," he said aloud. "It's that damn devil in there. He scraped me off. I'm not yellow." He was almost sobbing. The rifle fell from his shoulder. "How can I be yellow, all the tough broncs I've topped!" he screamed at himself.

The misery and shame combined with the rage that remained in him still. "Damn you," he cried at the roan, and began to slide between the poles into the corral. "I'll show you if I'm yellow. You scrape me off again and I'll put a slug through your brain!"

He ran up to the roan in a frenzy and made a grab for the reins, but the horse whirled and galloped away. Half-blind with fury, panting, cursing, sobbing, Travis snatched his rope and went after the roan. He cornered it and dropped the loop over its neck and then, hand over hand, he went swiftly up to the lunging, plunging animal.

The roan started to rear, but Travis had a good hold on the hackamore and he wouldn't let go. The roan snorted and swung away, but Travis, raging, hung on. He made a wild, leaping grab for the saddle horn and caught it and went up into the saddle.

The roan, squealing with fury, was pitching and lunging even before Travis hit the kak. The jolt of it cracked his teeth together, but he stayed on and caught up the lines and found the flapping stirrups with his boots.

The roan was in the full grip of its fury as it went bucking savagely across the corral. Travis didn't expect to stay on. He hadn't guessed that the roan could be so savage. Those other attempts had been picnics compared to this try. He expected to be thrown momentarily.

Realizing that defeat was imminent, the rage in Travis grew. As the jolts jarred him, he began to scream, "Go on, pitch me off. Throw me, damn you! Throw me and I'll put a slug in your brain!"

He was sobbing with anger. Stinging tears ran down his cheeks. He thought it might be blood, but he knew better: it was only his cowardice that made him think it was blood running out of his nose and mouth.

"Pitch me off," he screamed at the roan. "Throw me. The gun is ready for you, you damn devil. Throw me!"

The roan aimed for the side of the corral, but Travis saw it coming and he swung his leg out of the way and stayed on the roan with only one foot in a stirrup to support him. The horse smashed with insane fury against the poles and rebounded and Travis settled back in the kak again. His spurs raked the roan's flanks.

"Throw me," he shouted, knowing he didn't have long to go. "Pitch me off, you red devil. You'll throw me just once more. I promise you that!"

The wetness on his face tasted like blood, but he knew it was just his cowardice playing tricks on him. He knew he would never conquer this fear. Once he went off the roan he would never mount another bucker. Travis was sobbing openly now.

"Throw me!" he shouted. "What you waiting for? Damn it, come on and throw me!"

The roan squealed and reared high and for a breathtaking instant trembled there, then came crashing down on its back. But Travis had kicked free of the stirrups and was down on the ground as the roan crashed on its back. It was instinct more than anything else that sent Travis back into the saddle as the roan righted itself and lunged up on its feet. It started to rear again and Travis raked hard with the spurs and sawed on the lines, and this time the roan did not crash over backward. It came down on its four hoofs and started crow-hopping.

"Throw me," Travis croaked. "Pitch me off, you devil. Throw me!"

Finally it dawned on Travis that the jolts were not so hard anymore. The roan's fury seemed to have diminished. Its stiff-legged hopping was half-hearted, but Travis couldn't believe that he had triumphed.

The roan tried two more desultory hops and then brought up still, legs spraddled, foam-flecked flanks heaving. Travis could hear the whistling of the roan's breath and he lifted a hand to wipe the sweat off his face and he saw it was really blood that was running out of his nose.

Travis awoke and saw that it was evening. He rose, fully clothed, from his bunk and went outside. He was still sore from the effects of his ride, but it was a good stiffness. For the first time in more than a year he felt at peace with himself.

He walked slowly down to the corral. The roan was standing listless, as if it, too, were fully spent. Travis stood and stared at the roan and he began to feel something inside that he couldn't put into words. He guessed it was gratitude, and then he started to think it was more than that.

The roan turned its head once and looked at Travis. Then it dropped its head and just stood there. It no longer was a proud, untamed animal. Its spirit was broken, as Travis's had almost been broken. The roan would make a good mount, Travis thought, but its fight was gone forever.

Travis wondered then if it had really been worth it.

Before he turned to writing superior crime novels (Fifty-Two Pickup, City Primeval, Cat Chaser), Elmore Leonard specialized in Western fiction. Among his novels in this field are Hombre, considered by many to be one of the ten or fifteen best Westerns of the past quarter-century, The Bounty Hunters, Valdez Is Coming, and Forty Lashes Less One. Among his short stories are "Three Ten To Yuma," which was made into the classic film starring Van Heflin and Glenn Ford. "The Nagual," which has never before been reprinted, is another of his fine short stories—the powerful tale of a vaquero named Ofelio Oso.

The Nagual

Elmore Leonard

Ofelio Oso—*who had been a* vaquero *most of his seventy* years, but who now mended fences and drove a wagon for John Stam—looked down the slope through the jack pines seeing the man with his arms about the woman. They were in front of the shack which stood near the edge of the deep ravine bordering the west end of the meadow; and now Ofelio watched them separate lingeringly, the woman moving off, looking back as she passed the corral, going diagonally across the pasture to the trees on the far side where she disappeared.

Now Mrs. Stam goes home, Ofelio thought, to wait for her husband.

The old man had seen them like this before, sometimes in the evening, sometimes at dawn as it was now with the first distant sun streak off beyond the Organ Mountains, and always when

John Stam was away. This had been going on for months now, at least since Ofelio first began going up into the hills at night.

It was a strange feeling that caused the old man to do this; more an urgency, for he had come to a realization that there was little time left for him. In the hills at night a man can think clearly, and when a man believes his end is approaching there are many things to think about.

In his sixty-ninth year Ofelio Oso broke his leg. In the shock of a pain-stabbing moment it was smashed between horse and corral post as John Stam's cattle rushed the gate opening. He could no longer ride, after having done nothing else for more than fifty years; and with this came the certainty that his end was approaching. Since he was of no use to anyone, only death remained. In his idleness he could feel its nearness and he thought of many things to prepare himself for the day it would come.

Now he waited until the horsebreaker, Joe Slidell, went into the shack. Ofelio limped down the slope through the pines and was crossing a corner of the pasture when Joe Slidell reappeared, leaning in the doorway with something in his hand, looking absently out at the few mustangs off at the far end of the pasture. His gaze moved to the bay stallion in the corral, then swung slowly until he was looking at Ofelio Oso.

The old man saw this and changed his direction, going toward the shack. He carried a blanket over his shoulder and wore a willow-root Chihuahua hat, and his hand touched the brim of it as he approached the loose figure in the doorway.

"At it again," Joe Slidell said. He lifted the bottle which he held close to his stomach and took a good drink. His face contorted and he grunted, "Yaaaaa!" but after that he seemed relieved. He nodded to the hill and said, "How long you been up there?"

"Through the night," Ofelio answered. Which you well know, he thought. You, standing there drinking the whiskey that the woman brings.

Slidell wiped his mouth with the back of his hand, watching the old man through heavy-lidded eyes. "What do you see up there?"

"Many things."

"Like what?"

Ofelio shrugged. "I have seen devils."

Slidell grinned. "Big ones or little ones?"

"They take many forms."

Joe Slidell took another drink of the whiskey, not offering it to the old man, then said, "Well, I got work to do." He nodded to the corral where the bay stood looking over the rail, lifting and shaking his maned head at the man smell. "That horse," Joe Slidell said, "is going to finish gettin' himself broke today, one way or the other."

Ofelio looked at the stallion admiringly. A fine animal for long rides, for the killing pace, but for cutting stock, no. It would never be trained to swerve inward and break into a dead run at the feel of boot touching stirrup. He said to the horse breaker, "That bay is much horse."

"Close to seventeen hands," Joe Slidell said, "if you was to get close enough to measure."

"This is the one for Señor Stam's use?"

Slidell nodded. "Maybe. If I don't ride him down to the house before supper, you bring up a mule to haul his carcass to the ravine." He jerked his thumb past his head indicating the deep draw behind the shack. Ofelio had been made to do this before. The mule dragged the still faintly breathing mustang to the ravine edge. Then Slidell would tell him to push, while he levered with a pole, until finally the mustang went over the side down the steep-slanted seventy feet to the bottom.

Ofelio crossed the pasture, then down into the woods that fell gradually for almost a mile before opening again at the house and outbuildings of John Stam's spread. That *jinete*—that breaker of horses—is very sure of himself, the old man thought, moving through the trees. Both with horses and another man's wife. He must know I have seen them together, but it doesn't bother him. No, the old man thought now, it is something other than being sure of himself. I think it is stupidity. An intelligent man tames a wild horse with a great deal of respect, for he knows the horse is able to kill him. As for Mrs. Stam, considering her husband one would think he would treat her with even greater respect.

Marion Stam was on the back porch while Ofelio hitched the mules to the flatbed wagon. Her arms were folded across her chest and she watched the old man because his hitching the team was the only activity in the yard. Marion Stam's eyes were listless, darkly shadowed, making her thin face seem transparently frail and this made her look older than her twenty-five years. But appearance made little difference to Marion. John Stam was nearly twice her age; and Joe Slidell—Joe spent all his time up at the horse camp, anything in a dress looked good to him.

But the boredom. This was the only thing to which Marion Stam could not resign herself. A house miles away from no-where. Day following day, each one utterly void of anything resembling her estimation of living. John Stam at the table, his eyes on his plate, opening his mouth only to put food into it. The picture of John Stam at night, just before blowing out the lamp, standing in his yellowish, musty-smelling long under-wear. "Good night," a grunt, then the sound of even, open-mouthed breathing. Joe Slidell relieved some of the boredom. Some. He was young, not bad-looking in a coarse way, but Lord, he smelled like one of his horses!

"Why're you going now?" she called to Ofelio. "The stage's always late."

The old man looked up. "Someday it will be early. Perhaps this morning."

The woman shrugged, leaning in the door frame now, her arms still folded over her thin chest as Ofelio moved the team and wagon creaking out of the yard.

But the stage was not early; nor was it on time. Ofelio urged the mules into the empty station yard and pulled to a slow stop in front of the wagon shed that joined the station adobe. Two horses were in the shed with their muzzles munching at the hay-rack. Spainhower, the Butterfield agent, appeared in the door-way for a moment. Seeing Ofelio he said, "Seems you'd learn to leave about thirty minutes later." He turned away.

Ofelio smiled, climbing off the wagon box. He went through the door following Spainhower into the sudden dimness, feel-

ing the adobe still cool from the night and hearing a voice saying: "If Ofelio drove for Butterfield nobody'd have to wait for
stages." He recognized the voice and the soft laugh that followed and then he saw the man, Billy-Jack Trew, sitting on one
end of the pine table with his boots resting on a Douglas chair.

Billy-Jack Trew was a deputy. Val Dodson, his boss, the
Dona Ana sheriff, sat a seat away from him with his elbows on
the pine boards. They had come down from Tularosa, stopping
for a drink before going on to Mesilla.

Billy-Jack Trew said in Spanish, "Ofelio, how does it go?"

The old man nodded. "I passes well," he said and smiled,
because Billy-Jack was a man you smiled at even though you
knew him slightly and saw him less than once in a month.

"Up there at that horse pasture," the deputy said, "I hear
Joe Slidell's got some mounts of his own."

Ofelio nodded. "I think so. Señor Stam does not own all of
them."

"I'm going to take me a ride up there pretty soon," Billy-
Jack said, "and see what kind of money Joe's askin'. Way the
sheriff keeps me going I need two horses, and that's a fact."

Ofelio could feel Spainhower looking at him, Val Dodson
glancing now and then. One or the other would soon ask about
his nights in the hills. He could feel this also. Everyone seemed
to know about his going into the hills and everyone continued to
question him about it, as if it were a foolish thing to do. Only
Billy-Jack Trew would talk about it seriously.

At first, Ofelio had tried to explain the things he thought about:
life and death and man's place, the temptations of the devil and
man's obligation to God—all those things men begin to think
about when there is little time left. And from the beginning
Ofelio saw that they were laughing at him. Serious faces
straining to hold back smiles. Pseudosincere questions that
were only to lead him on. So after the first few times he stopped
telling them what occurred to him in the loneliness of the night
and would tell them whatever entered his mind, though much of
it was still fact.

Billy-Jack Trew listened, and in a way he understood the old man. He knew that legends were part of a Mexican peon's life. He knew that Ofelio had been a *vaquero* for something like fifty years, with lots of lonesome time for imagining things. Anything the old man said was good listening, and a lot of it made sense after you thought about it awhile—so Billy-Jack Trew didn't laugh.

With a cigar stub clamped in the corner of his mouth, Spainhower's puffy face was dead serious looking at the old man. "Ofelio," he said. "This morning there was a mist ring over the gate. Now I heard what that meant, so I kept my eyes open and sure'n hell here come a gang of elves through the gate dancin' and carryin' on. They marched right in here and hauled theirselves up on that table." ·

Val Dodson said dryly, "Now that's funny, just this morning coming down from Tularosa me and Billy-Jack looked up to see this be-ootiful she-devil running like hell for a cholla clump." He paused, glancing at Ofelio. "Billy-Jack took one look and was half out his saddle when I grabbed him."

Billy-Jack Trew shook his head. "Ofelio, don't mind that talk."

The old man smiled, saying nothing.

"You seen any more devils?" Spainhower asked him.

Ofelio hesitated, then nodded, saying, "Yes, I saw two devils this morning. Just at dawn."

Spainhower said, "What'd they look like?"

"I know," Val Dodson said quickly.

"Aw, Val," Billy-Jack said. "Leave him alone." He glanced at Ofelio, who was looking at Dodson intently, as if afraid of what he would say next.

"I'll bet," Dodson went on, "they had horns and hairy, forked tails like that one me and Billy-Jack saw out on the sands." Spainhower laughed, then Dodson winked at him and laughed too.

Billy-Jack Trew was watching Ofelio and he saw the tense expression on the old man's face relax. He saw the half-frightened look change to a smile of relief, and Billy-Jack was thinking that maybe a man ought to listen even a little closer to what Ofelio said. Like maybe there were double meanings to the things he said.

"Listen," Ofelio said, "I will tell you something else I have seen. A sight few men have ever witnessed." Ofelio was thinking: All right, give them something for their minds to work on.

"What I saw is a very hideous thing to behold, more frightening than elves, more terrible than devils." He paused, then said quietly, "What I saw was a *nagual.*"

He waited, certain they had never heard of this, for it was an old Mexican legend. Spainhower was smiling, but half-squinting curiosity was in his eyes. Dodson was watching, waiting for him to go on. Still, Ofelio hesitated and finally Spainhower said, "And what's a *nagual* supposed to be?"

"A *nagual,*" Ofelio explained carefully, "is a man with strange powers. A man who is able to transform himself into a certain animal."

Spainhower said, too quickly, "What kind of an animal?"

"That," Ofelio answered, "depends upon the man. The animal is usually of his choice."

Spainhower's brow was deep furrowed. "What's so terrible about that?"

Ofelio's face was serious. "One can see you have never beheld a *nagual.* Tell me, what is more hideous, what is more terrible than a man—who is made in God's image—becoming an animal?"

There was silence. Then Val Dodson said, "Aw—"

Spainhower didn't know what to say; he felt disappointed, cheated.

And into this silence came the faint rumbling sound. Billy-Jack Trew said, "Here she comes." They stood up, moving for the door, and soon the rumble was higher pitched—creaking, screeching, rattling, pounding—and the Butterfield stage was swinging into the yard. Spainhower and Dodson and Billy-Jack Trew went outside, Ofelio and his *nagual* forgotten.

No one had ever seen John Stam smile. Some, smiling themselves, said Marion must have at least once or twice, but most doubted even this. John Stam worked hard, twelve to sixteen hours a day, plus keeping a close eye on some business interests he had in Mesilla, and had been doing it since he'd first visually staked off his range six years before. No one asked where he came from and John Stam didn't volunteer any answers.

Billy-Jack Trew said Stam looked to him like a red dirt farmer with no business in cattle, but that was once Billy-Jack was wrong and he admitted it himself later. John Stam appeared one day with a crow-bait horse and twelve mavericks including a bull. Now, six years later, he had himself way over a thousand head and a *jinete* to break him all the horses he could ride.

Off the range, though, he let Ofelio Oso drive him wherever he went. Some said he felt sorry for Ofelio because the old Mexican had been a good hand in his day. Others said Marion put him up to it so that she wouldn't have Ofelio hanging around the place all the time. There was always some talk about Marion, especially now with the cut-down crew up at the summer range, John Stam gone to tend his business about once a week and only Ofelio and Joe Slidell there. Joe Slidell wasn't a bad-looking man.

The first five years, John Stam allowed himself only two pleasures: he drank whiskey, though no one had ever seen him drinking it, only buying it; and every Sunday afternoon he'd ride to Mesilla for dinner at the hotel. He would always order the same thing, chicken, and always sit at the same table. He had been doing this for some time when Marion started waiting table there. Two years later, John Stam asked her to marry him as she was setting down his dessert and Marion said yes then and there. Some claimed the only thing he'd said to her before that was bring me the ketchup.

Spainhower said it looked to him like Stam was from a line of hardheaded Dutchmen. Probably his dad had made him work like a mule and never told him about women, Spainhower said, so John Stam never knew what it was like *not* to work, and the first woman he looked up long enough to notice, he married. About everybody agreed Spainhower had something.

They were almost to the ranch before John Stam spoke. He had nodded to the men in the station yard, but gotten right up on the wagon seat. Spainhower asked him if he cared for a drink, but he shook his head. When they were in view of the ranch house—John Stam's leathery mask of a face looking straight ahead down the slope—he said, "Mrs. Stam is in the house?"

"I think so," Ofelio said, looking at him quickly then back to the rumps of the mules.

"All morning?"

"I was not here all morning." Ofelio waited, but John Stam said no more. This was the first time Ofelio had been questioned about Mrs. Stam. Perhaps he overheard talk in Mesilla, he thought.

In the yard, John Stam climbed off the wagon and went into the house. Ofelio headed the team for the barn and stopped before the wide door to unhitch. The yard was quiet; he glanced at the house, which seemed deserted, though he knew John Stam was inside. Suddenly Mrs. Stam's voice was coming from the house, high-pitched, excited, the words not clear. The sound stopped abruptly and it was quiet again. A few minutes later the screen door slammed and John Stam was coming across the yard, his great gnarled hands hanging empty, threateningly at his sides.

He stopped before Ofelio and said bluntly, "I'm asking you if you've ever taken any of my whiskey."

"I have never tasted whiskey," Ofelio said and felt a strange guilt come over him in this man's gaze. He tried to smile. "But in the past I've tasted enough mescal to make up for it."

John Stam's gaze held. "That wasn't what I asked you."

"All right," Ofelio said. "I have never taken any."

"I'll ask you once more," John Stam said.

Ofelio was bewildered. "What would you have me say?"

For a long moment John Stam stared. His eyes were hard, though there was a weariness in them. He said, "I don't need you around here, you know."

"I have told the truth," Ofelio said simply.

The rancher continued to stare, a muscle in his cheek tightening and untightening. He turned abruptly and went back to the house.

The old man thought of the times he had seen Joe Slidell and

the woman together and the times he had seen Joe Slidell drinking the whiskey she brought to him. Ofelio thought: He wasn't
asking about whiskey, he was asking about his wife. But he
could not come out with it. He knows something is going on behind his back, or else he suspicions it strongly, and he sees a
relation between it and the whiskey that's being taken. I think I
feel sorry for him; he hasn't learned to keep his woman and he
doesn't know what to do.

Before supper, Joe Slidell came down out of the woods
trail on the bay stallion. He dismounted at the back porch
and he and John Stam talked for a few minutes, looking over
the horse. When Joe Slidell left, John Stam, holding the bridle, watched him disappear into the woods, and for a long
time after he stood there staring at the trail that went up
through the woods.

Just before dark, John Stam rode out of the yard on the bay
stallion. Later—it was full dark then—Ofelio heard the screen
door again. He rose from his bunk in the end barn stall and
opened the big door an inch in time to see Marion Stam's dim
form pass into the trees.

He has left, Ofelio thought, so she goes to the *jinete*. He
shook his head thinking: This is none of your business. But it
remained in his mind, and later with his blanket over his shoulder, he went into the hills where he could think of these things
more clearly.

He moved through the woods hearing the night sounds which
seemed far away and his own footsteps in the leaves that were
close but did not seem to belong to him; then he was on the pine
slope and high up he felt the breeze. For a time he listened to
the soft sound of it in the jack pines. Tomorrow there will be
rain, he thought. Sometime in the afternoon.

He stretched out on the ground, rolling the blanket behind his
head, and looked up at the dim stars thinking: More and more
every day, *viejo,* you must realize you are no longer of any
value. The horse breaker is not afraid of you, the men at the station laugh and take nothing you say seriously, and finally Señor
Stam, he made it very clear when he said, "I don't need you
around here."

Then why does he keep me—months now since I have been

dismounted—except out of charity? He is a strange man. I suppose I owe him something, something more than feeling sorry for him, which does him no good. I think we have something in common. I can feel sorry for both of us. He laughed at this and tried to discover other things they might have in common. It relaxed him, his imagination wandering, and soon he dozed off with the cool breeze on his face, not remembering to think about his end approaching.

To the east, above the chimneys of the Organ range, morning light began to gray-streak the day. Ofelio opened his eyes, hearing the horse moving through the trees below him: hooves clicking on the small stones and the swish of pine branches. He thought of Joe Slidell's mustangs. One of them has wandered up the slope. But then he heard the unmistakable squeak of saddle leather and he sat up, tensed. It could be anyone, he thought. Almost anyone.

He rose, folding the blanket over his shoulder, and made his way down the slope silently, following the sound of the horse, and when he reached the pasture he saw the dim shape of it moving toward the shack, a tall shadow gliding away from him in the half-light.

The door opened. Joe Slidell came out closing it quickly behind him. "You're up early," he said, yawning, pulling a suspender over his shoulder. "How's that horse carry you? He learned his manners yesterday . . . won't give you no trouble. If he does, you let me have him back for about an hour." Slidell looked above the horse to the rider. "Mr. Stam, why're you lookin' at me like that?" He squinted up in the dimness. "Mr. Stam, what's the matter? You feelin' all right?"

"Tell her to come out," John Stam said.

"What?"

"I said tell her to come out."

"Now, Mr. Stam—" Slidell's voice trailed off, but slowly a grin formed on his mouth. He said, almost embarrassedly, "Well, Mr. Stam, I didn't think you'd mind." One man talking to another now. "Hell, it's only a little Mex gal from Mesilla. It gets lonely here and—"

John Stam spurred the stallion violently; the great stallion lunged, rearing, coming down with thrashing hooves on the screaming man. Slidell went down covering his head, falling against the shack boards. He clung there gasping as the stallion backed off; the next moment he was crawling frantically, rising, stumbling, running; he looked back, saw John Stam spurring and he screamed again as the stallion ran him down. John Stam reined in a tight circle and came back over the motionless form. He dismounted before the shack and went inside.

Go away, quickly, Ofelio told himself, and started for the other side of the pasture, running tensed, not wanting to hear what he knew would come. But he could not outrun it, the scream came turning him around when he was almost to the woods.

Marion Stam was in the doorway, then running across the yard, swerving as she saw the corral suddenly in front of her. John Stam was in the saddle spurring the stallion after her, gaining as she followed the rail circle of the corral. Now she was looking back, seeing the stallion almost on top of her. The stallion swerved suddenly as the woman screamed going over the edge of the ravine.

Ofelio ran to the trees before looking back. John Stam had dismounted. He removed bridle and saddle from the bay and put them in the shack. Then he picked up a stone and threw it at the stallion, sending it galloping for the open pasture.

The old man was breathing in short gasps from the running, but he hurried now through the woods and did not stop until he reached the barn. He sat on the bunk listening to his heart, feeling it in his chest. Minutes later, John Stam opened the big door. He stood looking down at Ofelio while the old man's mind repeated: Mary, Virgin and Mother, until he heard the rancher say, "You didn't see or hear anything all night. I didn't leave the house, did I?"

Ofelio hesitated, then nodded slowly as if committing this to memory. "You did not leave the house."

John Stam's eyes held his threateningly before he turned and went out. Minutes later, Ofelio saw him leave the house with a shotgun under his arm. He crossed the yard and entered the woods. Already he is unsure, Ofelio thought, especially of the woman, though the fall was at least seventy feet.

When he heard the horse come down out of the woods it was barely more than an hour later. Ofelio looked out, expecting to see John Stam on the bay, but it was Billy-Jack Trew walking his horse into the yard. Quickly the old man climbed the ladder to the loft. The deputy went to the house first and called out. When there was no answer he approached the barn and called Ofelio's name.

He's found them! But what brought him? Ah, the old man thought, remembering, he wants to buy a horse. He spoke of that yesterday. But he found them instead. Where is Señor Stam? Why didn't he see him? He heard the deputy call again, but still Ofelio did not come out. He remained crouched in the darkness of the barn loft until he heard the deputy leave.

The door opened and John Stam stood below in the strip of outside light.

Resignedly Ofelio said, "I am here," looking down, thinking: He was close all the time. He followed the deputy back and if I had called he would have killed both of us. And he is very capable of killing.

John Stam looked up, studying the old man. Finally he said, "You were there last night; I'm sure of it now . . . else you wouldn't be hiding, afraid of admitting something. You were smart not to talk to him. Maybe you're remembering you owe me something for keeping you on, even though you're not good for anything." He added abruptly, "You believe in God?"

Ofelio nodded.

"Then," John Stam said, "swear to God you'll never mention my name in connection with what happened."

Ofelio nodded again, resignedly, thinking of his obligation to this man. "I swear it," he said.

The rain came in the later afternoon, keeping Ofelio inside the barn. He crouched in the doorway listening to the soft hissing of the rain in the trees, watching the puddles forming in the wagon tracks. His eyes would go to the house, picturing John Stam inside alone with his thoughts and waiting. They will come. Perhaps the rain will delay them, Ofelio thought, but they will come.

The sheriff will say, Mr. Stam, this is a terrible thing we have to tell you. What? Well, you know the stallion Joe Slidell was breaking? Well, it must have got loose. It looks like Joe tried to catch him and . . . Joe got under his hooves. And Mrs. Stam was there . . . we figured she was up to look at your new horse—saying this with embarrassment. She must have become frightened when it happened and she ran. In the dark she went over the side of the ravine. Billy-Jack found them this morning. . . .

He did not hear them because of the rain. He was staring at a puddle and when he looked up there was Val Dodson and Billy-Jack Trew. It was too late to climb to the loft.

Billy-Jack smiled. "I was around earlier, but I didn't see you." His hat was low, shielding his face from the light rain, as was Dobson's.

Ofelio could feel himself trembling. He is watching now from a window. Mother of God, help me.

Dodson said, "Where's Stam?"

Ofelio hesitated, then nodded toward the house.

"Come on," Dodson said. "Let's get it over with."

Billy-Jack Trew leaned closer, resting his forearm on the saddle horn. He said gently, "Have you seen anything more since yesterday?"

Ofelio looked up, seeing the wet, smiling face and another image that was in his mind—a great stallion in the dawn light—and the words came out suddenly, as if forced from his mouth. He said, "I saw a *nagual*!"

Dodson groaned, "Not again," and nudged his horse with his knees.

"Wait a minute," Billy-Jack said quickly. Then to Ofelio, "This *nagual*, you actually saw it?"

The old man bit his lips. "Yes."

"It was an animal you saw then."

"It was a *nagual*."

Dodson said, "You stand in the rain and talk crazy. I'm getting this over with."

Billy-Jack swung down next to the old man. "Listen a minute, Val." To Ofelio, gently again, "But it was in the form of an animal?"

Ofelio's head nodded slowly.

"What did the animal look like?"

"It was," the old man said slowly, not looking at the deputy, "a great stallion." He said quickly, "I can tell you no more than that."

Dodson dismounted.

Billy-Jack said, "And where did the *nagual* go?"

Ofelio was looking beyond the deputy toward the house. He saw the back door open and John Stam came out on the porch, the shotgun cradled in his arm. Ofelio continued to stare. He could not speak as it went through his mind: He thinks I have told them!

Seeing the old man's face, Billy-Jack turned, then Dodson.

Stam called, "Ofelio, come here!"

Billy-Jack said, "Stay where you are," and now his voice was not gentle. But the hint of a smile returned as he unfastened the two lower buttons of his slicker, and suddenly he called, "Mr. Stam! You know what a *nagual* is?" He opened the slicker all the way and drew a tobacco plug from his pants pocket.

Dodson whispered hoarsely, "What's the matter with you?"

Billy-Jack was smiling. "I'm only askin' a simple question."

John Stam did not answer. He was staring at Ofelio.

"Mr. Stam," Billy-Jack Trew called, "before I tell you what a *nagual* is I want to warn you I can get out a Colt a helluva lot quicker than you can swing a shotgun."

Ofelio Oso died at the age of ninety-three on a ranch outside Tularosa. They said about him he sure told some tall ones—about devils, and about seeing a *nagual* hanged for murder in Mesilla . . . whatever that meant . . . but he was much man.

Even at his age the old son relied on no one, wouldn't let a soul do anything for him, and died owing the world not one plugged peso. And wasn't the least bit afraid to die, even though he was so old. He used to say, "Listen, if there is no way to tell when death will come, then why should one be afraid of it?"

Native Texan Elmer Kelton has won three Spur Awards for Best Novel of the Year from the Western Writers of America for The Buffalo Wagons *(1956),* The Day the Cowboys Quit *(1970), and* The Time It Never Rained *(1972). He is equally adept at the creation of powerful and evocative short stories. "Man on the Wagon Tongue," the account of a clash between a white cowboy named Hall Jernigan and a black one named Coley Dawes, is among the best of these.*

Man on the Wagon Tongue

Elmer Kelton

One of the first things Hall Jernigan did after he joined the West Texas wagon crew of old Major Steward's M Bar outfit was to develop a strong dislike for Coley Dawes.

The reason? Well, it wasn't anything a man would be proud to admit, but the dislike was real, chafing like chapped skin rubbing against a saddle. Maybe the main thing was just that Coley Dawes was there, and his presence was an affront to a man of Hall's upbringing. Besides, Coley was just too blamed good at everything.

In the six weeks Hall had been with the wagon crew, he had seen Coley ride any number of pitching broncs, and he hadn't seen him thrown but once.

What really got Hall's hackles up was the morning when a bronc in his own string threw him off twice. Old Major March Steward rode up, scowling, as Hall swayed, gasping, to his feet the second time.

"Coley," the major said crisply, "you get up there and top off that bronc for this boy, will you?"

The word *boy* had done it, for Hall was a grown man and proud to say so. But the breath was gone from him, and the only protest he could make was a wild waving of his arms. Coley rode that bronc and made it look easy. When Coley got down from the saddle, the fight was out of the horse. It was *Hall* who wanted to fight. But there was the old major, sitting yonder on his horse and looking fierce as an eagle perched over a baby lamb. A glance at those sharp eyes and that graying beard made Hall choke down whatever he had started to say.

It wasn't fitten for a boss to put somebody else on a man's bronc that way and shame him. But the major was running a cow outfit, not a school in range etiquette. The roundup wouldn't wait for some cowpuncher who couldn't stay on. Some of those old mossy-horns like Major Steward were a lot more interested in getting cattle worked than in sparing some cowboy's wounded pride. Cowboys came cheap.

Coley handed Hall the reins and stepped back without a word. But try as he might, Coley couldn't keep the smile out of his eyes. He had been proud to do something the white man couldn't.

For Coley's skin was as black as a moonless night in May.

Maybe one reason Hall had held his silence so long was that the other cowboys accepted Coley and rode alongside him as if he were the same as the rest of them. The only time you could tell his color meant anything was around the wagon at night and at mealtime. Coley always toted his bedroll out to the edge of camp, a little apart from the others. Come mealtime, he waited till last to take his plate, and he always sat on the wagon tongue, to himself. Nobody had ever told him he had to, and likely no one would have said anything to him if he hadn't. But he had spent his boyhood in slavery. He would carry the mark of that even to the grave. He remembered, and he presumed little.

The way the other cowboys told it to Hall, Coley had been a lanky, half-starved kid of maybe fifteen when the war ended. The Yankees had told him he was free, but they must have meant just free to starve. Nobody wanted him. Nobody had a home for him, or any work. One day Major Steward had come across the ragged, pathetic button and had felt compassion. Steward was a little lank himself in those days, just beginning to build what was later to become a huge herd of cattle. But he picked up the boy and found something for him to do. With the major's coaching and his own natural ability, Coley had made himself a first-class cowboy. Many Negroes did, in those days.

When you came right down to it, maybe that was what rankled Hall Jernigan the most. Hall had learned his cowboying the hard way. His diploma had been several scars, a couple of knocked-down knuckles and a broken leg that had almost but not quite healed back straight. All this before he was twenty-three. And here was Coley Dawes several years older with no visible scars of the trade. Coley could ride, and he could rope. Up to now Hall hadn't found a thing he could do that Coley couldn't do just a little better.

It wasn't fitten. Broke though he was, Hall made up his mind he was going to ask for his time and leave this haywire outfit.

He caught the old major by the branding-iron fire, watching the irons turn a searing red. Scowling, Steward drew his thick fingers down through his ragged, dusty beard. "It's on account of Coley Dawes, I reckon. I been seein' it come on. Coley don't mean you any harm."

"Mean it or not, he's done it."

"Leave now and you're admittin' he's the better man."

Hotly Hall said, "I'm admittin' no such of a thing."

"Aren't you?" The major's eyebrows drew down, and his eyes seemed to burn a hole through Hall. When Steward stared like that, most men started looking for something to get behind. "The only thing you've got against Coley is his color, ain't that right? If he was white like the rest of us, you'd pass it over and not get the ringtail just because he's better than you."

Hall clenched his fist. "I ain't said he's better . . ." He broke off, knowing that indirectly he had. The major had a way of cutting through the foliage and getting right to the trunk.

Hall shrugged, somehow wanting to explain. "I reckon it's just that I never did have no use for his kind. I growed up in Georgia. The rich plantation people called us 'poor white trash.' We never owned no slaves, never hoped to. War came, mostly on account of the slaves. Rich landowners up the road had a hundred of them, and my pa had to go to war to try and keep them from losin' their darkeys. Them rich plantation folks sat at home while Pa went and got hisself killed. There was seven of us kids, me the oldest, and just Ma to try and feed us. We like to've starved. Them rich folks up the road, they never gave us so much as a fat shoat. just sat there and held those slaves till the end, till old Sherman come. All that misery on account of them slaves. That's why I never had no use for a black man. They've caused too much misery. When I see one, I remember Pa and all them hungry days.''

Major Steward nodded. ''Looks to me like you misplaced your hatred. Those slaves, they were caught in the middle same as you.''

Hall shrugged. ''If it hadn't been for them, there wouldn't of been no war. I can't help how I feel. I'd be obliged if you'd just pay me and let me ride on.''

The major shook his head. ''If you'll remember, I got you out of jail. I paid your fine and loaned you money to buy a new outfit. You haven't worked here long enough yet to pay out.''

Hall swore. It hadn't been fair, that deal in town. They'd been cheating him at poker, and he had called their hand at it. Seemed like the law sided with the gamblers, though, especially the one who had lost three teeth to Hall's hard fist.

''All right,'' Hall said reluctantly, ''I'll stay long enough to get even. Till then, major, I'll thank you to keep that Coley out of my way.''

So Hall stayed on, and Coley Dawes gave him plenty of room. It bothered Hall sometimes, the way most of the cowboys associated freely with Coley, talking, joshing, acting almost as if he were white. But there was always that color mark: when mealtime came, Coley sat alone on the wagon tongue.

By and by the outfit had put a steer herd together, something like fifteen hundred of them. From somewhere east came a pair of buyers with a whole trail outfit of cowboys, ready to push the steers up the trail to Kansas. Hall Jernigan was at the wagon the day the final tally had been finished and the buyers paid off the major in cold cash. They had brought it with them in a canvas bag. With the bunch of cowboys they had along, nobody would have dared to try to take it. Hall got to wondering what the major was going to do with all that cash.

He didn't have to wonder long. That night the major called him over to the cook's fire. Steward was sipping a cup of coffee, and he made silent sign for Hall to do likewise.

"Hall," he said, "I got a special job for you. From what I heard in town about that fight that put you in jail, you're a right peart scrapper. And the boys tell me you're a crack shot."

Hall shrugged. "I can shoot some," he admitted.

"Most of these cowhands I got couldn't hit a barn from the inside. Dangerous, them even carryin' a gun around."

Hall sipped the steaming coffee and nodded agreement. Cowboys and loaded guns had always bothered him.

The major said, "I got a lot of cash on hand, and I need to get it to the bank in Fort Worth. Generally I take it myself, and nobody's ever had the nerve to try and steal it from me. But this time I got so much cow work left that I can't go. Got to send it with somebody I can trust."

Hall felt a glow of pride. "Thanks for the compliment."

"Don't thank me till I tell you about the rest of the job. I always take a man with me on my money trips. Even send him by himself when there's not much of it and I figure there's no risk. He knows all the ropes, but I wouldn't call him a fighter."

"I'll take care of him for you."

Major Steward brought his gaze down level with Hall's eyes. "You'd better. I'm talkin' about Coley Dawes."

"Coley?" Hall stiffened. "You mean you'd ask me to ride with that darkey all the way to Fort Worth?" He threw out his coffee and stomped around the fire a couple of times, his face clouded as if the major had asked him to spit on the Confederate flag. "Hell, no! Git yourself somebody else!"

"Got nobody else I'd send. I'll cancel out whatever you still owe me, Hall. Even give you fifty dollars extra bonus to fetch that money clear through to Forth Worth."

Fifty dollars! Hall paused to reflect. For that much he would almost shake hands with General Sherman.

Sharply he said, "Seems to me you're puttin' a heap of trust

in Coley. How do you know he won't take your money someday and just run off with it?''

"First place, he's too simple and honest. The thought probably never would enter his head. Second place, what could he do
with it? Anybody would know he had no business with that
kind of money. He couldn't spend it.''

"How do you know I won't take your money and run with it?''

A twinkle of humor flickered in the rancher's eyes, one of the
few Hall had seen in all the weeks he had worked here. "Same
reason. You've got too much of a cowhand look about you.
Anybody could tell you couldn't have come by that much
money honest.''

Hall flinched. He had asked for that, and he had gotten it.

Hall hadn't accepted, but the major plowed right on as if as-
suming there was no doubt about it. "One more thing: Coley
knows his way around, so he's boss on this trip. You do what
he says.''

"*Me*, take orders from Coley?'' It was unheard of, a thing
like that.

"You'll do what he says or you'll answer to me.''

Hall stalked off, talking under his breath. The things a man
would submit to, just to get out of debt.

The stars were still out crystal-sharp when Hall Jernigan and
Coley Dawes finished breakfast and headed eastward away
from the chuckwagon. Old Major Steward had taken Hall off to
one side and had spoken quietly. "Coley would die before he'd
let anybody get hold of them saddlebags. It's your job to see he
don't have to.''

From the beginning Hall had made it clear he didn't care to
do any jawing with Coley's kind, so Coley quietly hung back
and didn't say a word. Hall thought perhaps the Negro was riding along asleep, but when he looked back he saw the man's
eyes thoughtfully appraising him. It wasn't hard to guess what
was running through Coley's mind, for a quiet resentment
showed plain and open.

Hall turned back, shrugging. Didn't make any difference, he
told himself, what the likes of Coley thought of him.

They rode along silently hour after hour, and the quiet began to get on Hall's nerves. He had thought, before they started, that Coley would probably wear a man's ear down to a nub with useless talk. But the only time Coley opened his mouth was to spit out a little dust. Time came when Hall wanted to loosen up and talk a little. He would turn in the saddle and try to stàrt a conversation. All he got was a coldly polite "Yes, sir," or "No, sir," to his questions.

Patience wearing thin, Hall finally growled, "Well, don't just hang back there behind me. We're not a couple of Indians that we got to go single file."

Coley's teeth flashed in a momentary smile, then he caught himself and forced the smile away. The smile somehow brought up fresh anger in Hall. Suddenly he lost his wish for talk. Coley had won again. He always did, seemed like.

They jogged along in a steady trot all that day. A while before sundown they stopped to cook a little supper. That done, they moved on and didn't stop till dark. Hall had kept a good watch all day and hadn't seen a sign of anybody or anything suspicious. But when you carried enough money to start a new bank with, it didn't pay to advertise.

They didn't see anything notable the second day, either. In the afternoon they turned into a well-worn wagon road that meandered in a more or less easterly direction. "This here trail," Coley volunteered, "will take us to Fort Worth by and by."

That was almost the only thing the Negro had said the whole two days. Hall had given up trying to lure him into conversation. Hall came to realize that Coley had a strong pride, and Hall had injured it.

What does he think he is? Hall thought angrily. *A white man?*

Late in the afternoon Coley reined his horse off the trail. "Settlement up yonder a little ways," he said. "The major and me, we always cuts out around it when we got money with us. Major says most folks down there is honest, and he don't want to be givin' them no temptation that might cause them to stray."

Hall pulled his horse to a stop and eyed the trail speculatively. "Settlement, you say? Bound to have some drinkin' whiskey there, ain't they?" When Coley nodded, Hall rubbed his hand across his mouth. "By George, I got a thirst that would kill a mule."

"Mister Hall, we can't do that. We got to go on."

"It's comin' night. We got to stop someplace. We ain't seen no sign of trouble and I don't think we're goin' to. I'm thirsty."

Worry was in Coley's eyes. "Mister Hall, I know how you feels about me and all, and I know you don't favor my complexion none. But the major he done give us a job. We got to go to Fort Worth."

Coley's argument only firmed Hall's intentions.

"You can go to Fort Worth . . . even to hell if it suits you. I'm goin' to the settlement."

He touched spurs to his horse and rode on down the trail toward the settlement. He didn't look back to see what Coley was doing, but in a minute or two he heard the sound of Coley's horse following.

It wasn't much of a settlement, just a rude scattering of log-and-picket houses and a few small, frame buildings. Whole place probably couldn't roust out seventy-five people. Hall picked what was plainly a small saloon and stepped down in front of it. Looking back, he caught the sharp disapproval in Coley's eyes. It only strengthened his own resolve.

"You comin' in, Coley?"

"Them folks don't want me in there."

"Then I'll bring you a bottle. They won't mind you sittin' here on the front porch."

Coley's back was stiff. "I don't want no bottle. I reckon I'll just sit here and wait till you're ready to go."

It was a typical small-settlement saloon, one kerosene lamp giving it what little light it had. There obviously wasn't a broom on the premises, and the rough pine bar would leave splinters in a man if he dragged his arm across it. The whiskey was made to match. It tasted as bad as kerosene, but it had a jolt like the shod hoof of a Missouri mule. Hall paid twice what the bottle was worth and took it back to sit down at a table that rocked unevenly when he touched it. Each drink seemed to taste better than the one before it. Under the whiskey's rough glow he began losing the sense of degradation that had pressed down on him ever since he had left the major's chuckwagon.

This would show them, he told himself defiantly. They might make him ride with a Negro, but they couldn't make him take orders from one.

He had been in the place an hour or more when he became aware of rough voices out front.

"Turn around here to the light so we can see you, boy," someone was saying. Then, "You was right, Hob, it *is* the major's old pet Coley. What you doin' here, Coley? The old man must be around someplace, ain't he?"

Coley's voice was strained. "Mister Good, I ain't wantin' no trouble."

"We ain't fixin to give you none, Coley. But seein' you reminds us that a couple of cattle buyers was through here a few days ago with a bunch of cowboys on their way to get some stock off the major. And it strikes us that the only time you're ever away from the ranch is when you and the old man are a-carryin' money to the bank. So you tell us where he's at, Coley. Us boys want to pay him our respects."

"The major ain't here, and there ain't no money," Coley lied. "I done quit workin' for the major."

"Quit? A pet dog don't quit its master. And that's all you are—just a pet dog. Quit lyin' and tell us where the major's at. Tell us or we'll take the double of a rope to you."

Hall was suddenly cold sober. He pushed to his feet, knocking the bottle over. It rolled off the table, and whiskey gurgled out into the sawdust at his feet. Pistol in his hand, he pushed through the door and shoved the muzzle against the back of the nearest man's neck.

A startled gust of breath went out of the man at the touch of cold metal. Hall said, "You boys lookin' for trouble, you better come talk to me. Take your hands off of Coley before I do somethin' my conscience will plague me for."

The two men jerked away from Coley as if he had suddenly turned hot. Hall said, "Coley, you get on your horse."

Coley wasted no time. Hall's voice was brittle as he faced the pair. "Now, was there anything else you-all wanted to say?"

Neither man spoke. Hall said, "Next time you-all go to jump somebody, see if you've got the guts to take on a white man. Now git!"

They got.

Hall swung into the saddle. "Coley, I think it's time we moseyed."

Coley nodded. "Yes, sir, Mister Hall. High time."

They left town in a walk, for Hall didn't want to appear in a hurry. Out of sight, they spurred into a lope and held it awhile. When he felt his horse tiring, Hall pulled him down to a trot.

"Who were they, Coley?"

"They ain't no friends of the major, I'll guarantee you that. They're the Good brothers, and there sure ain't much good about them. Used to work for the major till he found out they was stealin' every maverick they could get a rope on. Major ran them off—said they was lucky he didn't just go and hang them." His face twisted in worry. "They'll be trailin' after us, I reckon. They smell a skunk in the woodpile, sure as sin."

Hall looked at Coley's bulging saddlebags, and shame came galling him. "My fault, Coley. I oughtn't to've gone to the settlement. Mostly I just did it to show I wasn't takin' no orders from you."

Coley shrugged. "Ain't no use shuttin' the barn door after the milk's spilt. If it's all the same to you, I think we better keep a-ridin'."

Hall said, "You're the boss."

They rode until at least midnight. They didn't even build a fire for coffee, for neither man doubted that the Good brothers were somewhere behind them. Knowing as much as they already did, the Goods would have to be stupid not to figure out the rest.

Hall and Coley were up and riding again by daylight. With luck, Hall figured, they might reach Fort Worth by night. Maybe with the long night's ride they had gotten a strong lead on the Goods anyway. He and Coley kept a sharp eye on the trail, both behind them and ahead. Once Coley, turning in the saddle, pulled up and said, "Mister Hall, behind us!"

Hall stopped and looked. "Nothin' back there, Coley."

"I'd of swore, Mister Hall . . ."

They waited a little but saw nothing. There wasn't even enough breeze to wave the grass. Coley admitted, "I could've been wrong, I reckon. I'm still a mite skittish."

Hall nodded, somehow satisfied. This, then, was *his* department. This was one place, at least, where the Negro couldn't outshine him.

Riding, Hall could see tension wearing on Coley. The dark man's eyes were wide, the whites showing more than Hall had ever seen. Again Coley called out, "Mister Hall . . ."

But when Hall turned, Coley was looking uphill and shaking his head. "Nothin'. Guess I didn't see nothin'. For a minute I'd of swore . . ."

A bullet snarled past Hall's face and thudded into the grass. A second later he heard the sharp slap of a rifle shot and saw powder smoke rise black from behind a bush up the hill. Automatically he brought his pistol up and fired an answering wild shot that didn't hit within twenty feet of target.

"Ride, Coley!" he shouted.

Spurring, he dropped the six-shooter back into its holster and pulled his saddle gun out of its scabbard beneath his leg. Ahead of him, Coley Dawes was leaning well forward and putting heels to his horse. Scared to death, Hall thought. The ground seemed to fly by beneath. Looking back over his shoulder, Hall could see a rider come out from behind the bush and spur into pursuit.

There were two of them, Hall thought. *Where's the other one at?*

Ahead of him he saw a dead tree. He slid his horse to a stop, jumped down, leaned the rifle barrel over the fork of the tree and took aim. As the rifle roared, the pursuing horse went head over heels, and its rider rolled in the grass.

Afoot, Hall thought, *he can't hurt us much.*

Coley had slowed up and was waiting for him. Hall remounted and caught up. "Real peart shootin'," Coley said.

"You just have to know your business, is all," Hall said as they rode on. "But we got no time to be a-pattin' ourselves on the back. There's still another one someplace."

No sooner had he spoken than he felt his own horse jerk under the impact of a bullet. Instinctively Hall kicked his feet out of the stirrups. He felt himself hurled forward, rifle in his hands. He slid on rough ground, his clothes ripping, the dead limb of a mesquite gashing his hide. But he was up again instantly, crouching, his anxious gaze sweeping the skyline.

He saw smoke in a thicket ahead. He raised the saddle gun and triggered a shot in that direction. An answering bullet whined by him.

At least now I know where he's at. And he can't get out of that thicket without me gettin' a lick at him.

"Coley," Hall shouted, "you take that money and get the hell out of here!"

Coley had pulled his horse up behind a big mesquite and was bending low, watching the thicket. "I can't just ride off and leave you here alone, Mister Hall, with two of them white trash a-shootin' at you."

"I got one afoot and one bottled up. Long's I'm here they can't go after you. Now git yourself gone."

"But Mister Hall . . ."

"Damn it, Coley, I got you into this, and I'm gettin' you out. Ride now before I nail your hide to the fence!"

Reluctantly Coley rode away. To cover him, Hall kept firing into the thicket. Coley got away clean.

Well, Hall thought, *Coley won't stop now till he's got clear to Fort Worth.*

For the first time, he looked back to where the first robber's horse had fallen. He could see the dead horse, but not the man.

Slippin' up on me. Hall knew he had to shift himself to a more advantageous position. Here he had a cutbank to protect him against fire from the man in the thicket, but his back was exposed. He looked toward his dead horse and wished he had the extra cartridges that were in his saddlebags. But to get them he would have to go out into the open, and maybe roll that horse over as well. No matter, he had another two or three shots left in the rifle. After that, there was still the six-shooter.

All he had to do was to stall the pair around till dark. By then Coley should reach Fort Worth. And in the darkness Hall could steal away unseen.

The only thing he dreaded was the long walk.

Ahead of him he could see a gully, where hillside runoff water had cut into the grass and soil and eroded an outlet. In that gully he could have protection from both front and rear.

Moreover, weeds had grown up on either side which would help hide him from view without keeping him from watching what the two robbers were up to.

He lay still, studying the ground a minute, estimating how long it would take him to run to the gully. A few seconds should do it. He took a firm grip on the saddle gun, steadied himself, then broke into the open.

He almost made it to the gully. Then a bullet cut through his leg, and he went sprawling. He tried desperately to push himself to his feet, but the leg wouldn't hold him. Another bullet thumped into the grass ahead of him. Suddenly his mouth was dry and his heart was racing.

He hadn't seriously thought they could hit him while he was running. But they had. Behind him he could hear a man afoot, moving fast. The robber whose horse he had killed was closing in on him.

Just ahead of him was a mesquite tree. Water had cut around the base of it, leaving a pile of drift on the off side which might give him some protection from the man behind him. The tree itself would shield him from the man in the thicket. Hall turned and fired a quick shot at the man who was trying to close with him. The man dove into the protection that Hall had abandoned only seconds before. That gave Hall time to crawl to the tree.

He quickly found the protection here was not as good as it had appeared. The drift was deep enough to protect him only so long as he kept his head down. The moment he raised his head up to take a shot, he was exposed to the man behind him. This way he had lost any advantage he might once have had over the man in the thicket.

Despair swept over him now as he realized he was boxed. All the man behind him had to do was fire to keep Hall's head down while the outlaw in the thicket calmly took his time and came out. He would be able to come up and put a bullet in Hall while Hall lay helpless, waiting for it.

It didn't take the two robbers long to figure this out, either. The one behind began firing sporadically at Hall's hiding place. The slugs thudded into the soft earth and showered Hall with dirt. Hall would raise up slightly and answer occasionally with a shot of his own, but he knew all the advantage was with the outlaws.

It wouldn't be long before they decided to close in and kill him, for they knew Coley was getting away.

The man behind waved his hat. That, Hall knew, was a signal. In a moment Hall heard hoofbeats. A horse was coming out of the thicket and running toward him. Hall carefully brought up the rifle. They might get him, but they wouldn't do it cheap. . . .

A bullet smacked into the earth at Hall's face, showering him with sand, half blinding him. He snapped a shot at the man behind him and realized with a sick heart that he had missed.

He knew he had just a moment left to live, but that moment was long enough for him to know the sick feeling of desperation and the cold hand of remorse. If he hadn't been so all-fired resentful of Coley . . . If he hadn't gone to that settlement . . .

The man behind him jumped up and came running, firing as he moved. Hall heard the hoofs pounding harder, coming from the thicket. He blinked the sand from his eyes and pushed up on one leg, knowing this would give the horseman a chance at him but knowing too that it was the only way he could get a clear shot at the man afoot.

He heard a man scream, and almost at the same time he heard a rifle shot from somewhere uphill. Then he had his bead, and he squeezed the trigger. He saw the outlaw in his sights drop to his knees. The man braced himself on one hand and tried to level the pistol he held. Hall levered another cartridge into the breech and fired again. The man went down hard that time, down to stay.

Hall spun around, hearing the horse almost upon him.

The horse was there, all right. It passed him and kept running, its saddle empty. The rider from the thicket lay out there in the grass, his legs twitching, one arm twisted crazily beneath him. Down the hill came another rider, rifle in hand.

Coley Dawes.

Coley caught the outlaw's horse and took Hall to a ranch house he knew of. He left him there while he rode on to Fort

Worth with the major's money. He stopped by briefly again on his way back to the Steward ranch, but Hall didn't get to talk to him. Right about then, Hall's fever was at its highest, and there wasn't any talk in him.

A couple of weeks later Hall rode up to the major's chuckwagon just at dinnertime and unsaddled. He limped over to the wagon and took a plate. He glimpsed Coley Dawes. As always, Coley sat alone, on the wagon tongue.

Hall got himself some beef and beans and stopped in front of Coley. Coley looked up with a grin. "Welcome back, Mister Hall. How's the leg?"

"Mendin' fair to middlin'. Ain't goin' to lose it." He frowned. "Coley, you never did say why you came back that day. You was supposed to keep runnin'."

"I couldn't just go off and leave you in that kind of a fix. I hid the money and went back to see if I could help."

"I'm sure tickled you did. But you never did tell me you could shoot like that."

"I don't recollect as you ever asked me. You didn't like it 'cause I could ride and rope. Figured you'd sure disappreciate it if you was to find out I could shoot, too."

"Coley, from now on I won't care what you beat me at."

Humor sparkled in Coley's eyes. "Care to try me some evenin' on a little hand of poker?"

Hall chuckled. He looked at the long wagon tongue and at the Negro who sat on it, all alone.

"Move over, Coley," he said, "and make a little room for me."

Like Theodore Sturgeon's story earlier in this anthology, "Markers" is a tale of two fence-riding cowboys and of confidences shared on a lonely night, with a tragically ironic twist at the end. But in theme and subject matter, it is a wholly different story. Bill Pronzini has published twenty-eight novels and more than two hundred fifty short stories, articles, and essays; among these are numerous Westerns, including the novels The Gallows Land *and* Starvation Camp, *and the short stories in each of the previous anthologies in this series,* The Lawmen *and* The Outlaws.

Markers

Bill Pronzini

Jack Bohannon and I had been best friends for close to a year, ever since he'd hired on at the Two Bar Cross, but if it hadn't been for a summer squall that came up while the two of us were riding fence, I'd never have found out about who and what he was. Or about the markers.

We'd been out two weeks, working the range southeast of Eagle Mountain. The fences down along there were in middling fair shape, considering the winter we'd had; Bohannon and I sported calluses from the wire cutters and stretchers, but truth to tell, we hadn't been exactly overworking ourselves. Just kind of moving along at an easy pace. The weather had been fine—cool crisp mornings, warm afternoons, sky scrubbed clean of clouds on most days—and it made you feel good just to be there in all that sweet-smelling open space.

As it happened, we were about two miles east of the Eagle Mountain line shack when the squall came up. Came up fast, too, along about three o'clock in the afternoon, the way a summer storm does sometimes in Wyoming Territory. We'd been planning to spend a night at the line shack anyway, to replenish our supplies, so as soon as the sky turned cloudy dark we lit a shuck straight for it. The rain started before we were halfway there, and by the time we raised the shack, the downpour was such that you couldn't see a dozen rods in front of you. We were both soaked in spite of our slickers; rain like that has a way of slanting in under any slicker that was ever made.

The shack was just a one-room sod building with walls coated in ashes-and-clay and a whipsawed wood floor. All that was in it was a pair of bunks, a table and two chairs, a larder, and a big stone fireplace. First things we did when we came inside, after sheltering the horses for the night in the lean-to out back, were to build a fire on the hearth and raid the larder. Then, while we dried off, we brewed up some coffee and cooked a pot of beans and salt pork. It was full dark by then and that storm was kicking up a hell of a fuss; you could see lightning blazes outside the single window, and hear thunder grumbling in the distance and the wind moaning in the chimney flue.

When we finished supper Bohannon pulled a chair over in front of the fire, and I sat on one of the bunks, and we took out the makings. Neither of us said much at first. We didn't have to talk to enjoy each other's company; we'd spent a fair lot of time together in the past year—working the ranch, fishing and hunting, a little mild carousing in Saddle River—and we had an easy kind of friendship. Bohannon had never spoken much about himself, his background, his people, but that was all right by me. Way I figured it, every man was entitled to as much privacy as he wanted.

But that storm made us both restless; it was the kind of night a man sooner or later feels like talking. And puts him in a mood to share confidences, too. Inside a half hour we were swapping stories, mostly about places we'd been and things we'd done and seen.

That was how we came to the subject of markers—grave markers, first off—with me the one who brought it up. I was telling about the time I'd spent a year prospecting for gold in the

California Mother Lode, before I came back home to Wyoming Territory and turned to ranch work, and I recollected the grave I'd happened on one afternoon in a rocky meadow south of Sonora. A mound of rocks, it was, with a wooden marker anchored at the north end. And on the marker was an epitaph scratched out with a knife.

"I don't know who done it," I said, "or how come that grave was out where it was, but that marker sure did make me curious. Still does. What it said was, 'Last resting place of D. R. Lyon. Lived and died according to his name.' "

I'd told that story a time or two before and it had always brought a chuckle, if not a horse laugh. But Bohannon didn't chuckle. Didn't say anything, either. He just sat looking into the fire, not moving, a quirly drifting smoke from one corner of his mouth. He appeared to be studying on something inside his head.

I said, "Well, *I* thought it was a mighty unusual marker, anyhow."

Bohannon still didn't say anything. Another ten seconds or so passed before he stirred—took a last drag off his quirly and tossed it into the fire.

"I saw an unusual marker myself once," he said then, quiet. His voice sounded different than I'd ever heard it.

"Where was that?"

"Nevada. Graveyard in Virginia City, about five years ago."

"What'd it say?"

"Said 'Here lies Adam Bricker. Died of hunger in Virginia City, August 1882.' "

"Hell. How could a man die of hunger in a town?"

"That's what I wanted to know. So I asked around to find out."

"Did you?"

"I did," Bohannon said. "According to the local law, Adam Bricker'd been killed in a fight over a woman. Stabbed by the woman's husband, man named Greenbaugh. Supposed to've been self-defense."

"If Bricker was stabbed, how could he have died of hunger?"

"Greenbaugh put that marker on Bricker's grave. His idea of humor, I reckon. Hunger Bricker died of wasn't hunger for food, it was hunger for the woman. Or so Greenbaugh claimed."

"Wasn't it the truth?"

"Folks I talked to didn't think so," Bohannon said. "Story was, Bricker admired Greenbaugh's wife and courted her some; she and Greenbaugh weren't living together and there was talk of a divorce. Nobody thought he trifled with her, though. That wasn't Bricker's way. Folks said the real reason Greenbaugh killed him was because of money Bricker owed him. Bricker's claim was that he'd been cheated out of it, so he refused to pay when Greenbaugh called in his marker. They had an argument, there was pushing and shoving, and when Bricker drew a gun and tried to shoot him, Greenbaugh used his knife. That was his story, at least. Only witness just happened to be a friend of his."

"Who was this Greenbaugh?"

"Gambler," Bohannon said. "Fancy man. Word was he'd cheated other men at cards, and debauched a woman or two—that was why his wife left him—but nobody ever accused him to his face except Adam Bricker. Town left him pretty much alone."

"Sounds like a prize son of a bitch," I said.

"He was."

"Men like that never get what's coming to them, seems like."

"This one did."

"You mean somebody cashed in his chips for him?"

"That's right," Bohannon said. "Me."

I leaned forward a little. He was looking into the fire, with his head cocked to one side, like he was listening for another rumble of thunder. It seemed too quiet in there, of a sudden, so I cleared my throat and smacked a hand against my thigh.

I said, "How'd it happen? He cheat you at cards?"

"He didn't have the chance."

"Then how . . . ?"

Bohannon was silent again. One of the burning logs slid off the grate and made a sharp cracking sound; the noise seemed to jerk him into talking again. He said, "There was a vacant lot a few doors down from the saloon where he spent most of his time. I waited in there one night, late, and when he came along, on his way to his room at one of the hotels, I stepped out and put my gun up to his head. And I shot him."

"My God," I said. "You mean you *murdered* him?"

"You could call it that."

"But damn it, man, why?"

"He owed me a debt. So I called in his marker."

"What debt?"

"Adam Bricker's life."

"I don't see—"

"I didn't tell you how I happened to be in Virginia City. Or how I happened to visit the graveyard. The reason was Adam Bricker. Word reached me that he was dead, but not how it happened, and I went there to find out."

"Why? What was Bricker to you?"

"My brother," he said. "My real name is Jack Bricker."

I got up off the bunk and went to the table and turned the lamp up a little. Then I got out my sack of Bull Durham, commenced to build another smoke. Bohannon didn't look at me; he was still staring into the fire.

When I had my quirly lit I said, "What'd you do after you shot Greenbaugh?"

"Got on my horse and rode out of there."

"You figure the law knows you did it?"

"Maybe. But the law doesn't worry me much."

"Then how come you changed your name? How come you traveled all the way up here from Nevada?"

"Greenbaugh had a brother, too," he said. "Just like Adam had me. He was living in Virginia City at the time and he knows I shot Greenbaugh. I've heard more than once that he's looking for me—been looking ever since it happened."

"So he can shoot you like you shot his brother?"

"That's right. I owe him a debt, Harv, same as Greenbaugh owed me one. One of these days he's going to find me, and when he does he'll call in his marker, same as I did."

"Maybe he won't find you," I said. "Maybe he's stopped looking by this time."

"He hasn't stopped looking. He'll never stop looking. He's a hardcase like his brother was."

"That don't mean he'll ever cross your trail—"

"No. But he will. It's just a matter of time."

"What makes you so all-fired sure?"

"A feeling I got," he said. "Had it ever since I heard he was after me."

"Guilt," I said, quiet.

"Maybe. I'm not a killer, not truly, and I've had some bad nights over Greenbaugh. But it's more than that. It's something I know is going to happen, like knowing the rain will stop tonight or tomorrow and we'll have clear weather again. Maybe because there are too many markers involved, if you take my meaning—the grave kind and the debt kind. One of these days I'll be dead because I owe a marker."

Neither of us had anything more to say that night. Bohannon—I couldn't seem to think of him as Bricker—got up from in front of the fire and climbed into his bunk, and when I finished my smoke I did the same. What he'd told me kept rattling around inside my head. It was some while before I finally got to sleep.

I woke up right after dawn, like I always do—and there was Bohannon, with his saddlebags packed and his bedroll under one arm, halfway to the door. Beyond him, through the window, I could see pale gray light and enough of the sky to make out broken clouds; the storm had passed.

"What the hell, Bohannon?"

"Time for me to move on," he said.

"Just like that? Without notice to anybody?"

"I reckon it's best that way," he said. "A year in one place is long enough—maybe too long. I was fixing to leave anyway, after you and me finished riding fence. That's why I went ahead and told you about my brother and Greenbaugh and the markers. Wouldn't have if I'd been thinking on staying."

I swung my feet off the bunk and reached for my Levi's. "It don't make any difference to me," I said. "Knowing what you done, I mean."

"Sure it does, Harv. Hell, why lie to each other about it?"

"All right. But where'll you go?"

He shrugged. "Don't know. Somewhere. Best if you don't know, best if I don't myself."

"Listen, Bohannon—"

"Nothing to listen to." He came over and put out his hand, and I took it, and there was the kind of feeling inside me I'd had as a button when a friend died of the whooping cough. "Been good knowing you, Harv," he said. "I hope you don't come across a marker someday with my name on it." And he was gone before I finished buttoning up my pants.

From the window I watched him saddle his horse. I didn't go outside to say a final word to him—there wasn't anything more to say; he'd been right about that—and he didn't look back when he rode out. I never saw him again.

But that's not the whole story, not by any means.

Two years went by without my hearing anything at all about Bohannon. Then Curly Polk, who'd worked with the two of us on the Two Bar Cross and then gone down to Texas for a while, drifted back our way for the spring roundup, and he brought word that Bohannon was dead. Shot six weeks earlier, in the Pecos River town of Santa Rosa, New Mexico.

But it hadn't been anybody named Greenbaugh who pulled the trigger on him. It had been a local cowpuncher, liquored up, spoiling for trouble; and it had happened over a spilled drink that Bohannon had refused to pay for. The only reason Curly found out about it was that he happened to pass through Santa Rosa on the very day they hung the puncher for his crime.

It shook me some when Curly told about it. Not because Bohannon was dead—too much time had passed for that—but because of the circumstances of his death. He'd believed, and believed hard, that someday he'd pay for killing Greenbaugh; that there were too many markers in his life and someday he'd die on account of one he owed. Well, he'd been wrong. And yet the strange thing, the pure crazy thing, was that he'd also been right.

The name of the puncher who'd shot him was Sam Marker.

Few writers have been able to present consistently the true-to-life characters and in-depth details of the Old West as well as Clay Fisher, one of the two well-known pseudonyms (the other is Will Henry) of California resident Henry W. Allen. He has won four Western Writers of America Spur Awards and a wide spectrum of critical and popular acclaim. "Isley's Stranger" is just one of the superior tales in his 1962 collec-tion, The Oldest Maiden Lady in New Mexico and Other Stories.

Isley's Stranger

Clay Fisher

He *rode a mule. He was middling tall, middling spare, mid-dling young. He wore a soft, dark curly beard. His bedroll was one thready army blanket wound round a coffee can, tin cup, plate, razor, camp ax, Bible, copy of the* Rubáiyát, *a mouth harp, some other few treasures of like necessity in the wilder-ness.*

Of course, Isley didn't see all those things when the drifter rode up to his fire that night on Wolf Mountain flats. They came out later, after Isley had asked him to light down and dig in, the same as any decent man would do with a stranger riding up on him out of the dark and thirty miles from the next shelter. Isley always denied that he was smote with Christian charity, sweet reason or unbounding brother love in issuing the invite. It was simply that nobody turns anybody away out on the Wyo-ming range in late fall. Not with a norther building over Tongue River at twilight and the wind beginning to snap like a trapped weasel come full dark. No, sir. Not, especially, when that somebody looks at you with eyes that would make a kicked hound seem happy, and asks only to warm his hands and hear a friendly voice before riding on.

Well, Isley had a snug place. Anyway, it was for a line rider working alone in that big country. Isley could tell you that holes were hard to find out there in the wide open. And this one he had was ample big for two, or so he figured.

It was a sort of outcrop of the base rock, making a three-sided room at the top of a long, rolling swell of ground about midway of the twenty-mile flats. It had been poled and sodded over by some riders before Isley, and was not the poorest place in that country to bed down by several. Oh, what the heck, it wasn't the Brown Hotel in Denver, nor even the Drover's in Cheyenne. Sure, the years had washed the roof sods. And, sure, in a hard rain you had to wear your hat tipped back to keep the drip from spiking you down the nape of your shirt collar. But the three rock sides were airtight and the open side was south-facing. Likewise, the old grass roof, seepy or not, still cut out ninety-and-nine percent of the wind. Besides, it wasn't raining that night, nor about to. Moreover, Isley was a man who would see the sun with his head in a charcoal sack during an eclipse. It wasn't any effort, then, for him to ease up off his hunkers, step around the fire, bat the smoke out of his eyes, grin shy and say:

"Warm your hands, hell, stranger; unrope your bedroll and move in!"

They hit it off from scratch.

While the wanderer ate the grub Isley insisted on fixing for him—eating wasn't exactly what he did with it, it was more like inhaling—the little K-Bar hand had a chance to study his company. Usually, Isley was pretty fair at sizing a man, but this one had him winging. Was he tall? No, he wasn't tall. Was he short, then? No, you wouldn't say he was exactly short either. Middling, that's what he was. What kind of a face, then? Long? Thin? Square? Horsey? Fine? Handsome? Ugly? No, none of these things, and all of them too. He just had a face. It was like his build, just middling. So it went; the longer Isley looked at him, the less he saw that he could hang a guess on. With one flicker of the fire he looked sissy as skim milk. Then, with the next, he looked gritty as fish eggs rolled in sand. Cock your head one way and the fellow seemed so helpless he couldn't drive nails in a snowbank. Cock it the other and he appeared like he might haul hell out of its shuck. Isley decided he wouldn't bet either way on him in a tight election. One thing was certain, though. And that thing Isley would take bets on all winter. This curly-bearded boy hadn't been raised on the short grass. He wouldn't know a whiffletree from a wagon tongue, or a whey-belly bull from a bred heifer. He was as out of place in Wyoming as a cow on a front porch.

Isley was somewhat startled, then, when his guest got down the final mouthful of beans, reached for a refill from the coffee-pot and said quietly:

"There's bad trouble hereabouts, is there not, friend?"

Well, there was for a fact, but Isley couldn't see how this fellow, who looked like an out-of-work schoolteacher riding a long ways between jobs, could know anything about *that* kind of trouble.

"How come you to know that?" he asked. "It sure don't look to me like trouble would be in your line. No offense, mind you, mister. But around here—well, put it this way—there ain't nobody looking up the trouble we got. Most of us does our best to peer over it, or around it. What's your stake in the Wolf Mountain War, pardner?"

"Is that what it's called?" the other said softly. Then, with that sweet-sad smile that lighted up his pale face like candle shine, "Isn't it wonderful what pretty names men can think up for such ugly things? *'The Wolf Mountain War.'* It has alliteration, poetry, intrigue, beauty—"

Isley began to get a little edgy. This bearded one he had invited in out of the wind was not quite all he ought to be, he decided. He had best move careful. Sometimes these nutty ones were harmless, other times they would kill you quicker than anthrax juice.

He tried sending a return smile with his reply.

"Well, yes, whatever you say, friend. It's just another fight over grass and water, whatever you want to call it for a name. There's them as has the range, and them as wants the range. It don't change none."

"Which side are you on, Isley?"

"Well, now, you might say that—" Isley broke off to stare at him. *"Isley?"* he said. "How'd you know my name?"

The stranger looked uncomfortable, just for a moment. ~~He~~ appeared to glance around as though stalling for a good answer. Then, he nodded and pointed to Isley's saddle propped against the rear wall.

"I read it on your stirrup fender, just now."

Isley frowned. He looked over at the saddle. Even knowing where he had worked in that *T-o-m I-s-l-e-y* with copperhead rivets and a starnose punch, he couldn't see it. It lay up under the fender on the saddle skirt about an inch or so, purposely put there so he could reveal it to prove ownership in case somebody borrowed it without asking.

"Pretty good eyes," he said to the stranger. "That's mighty small print considering it's got to be read through a quarter inch of skirting leather."

The stranger only smiled.

"The skirt is curled a little, Isley, and the rivets catch the firelight. Call it that, plus a blind-luck guess."

The small puncher was not to be put off.

"Well," he said, "if you're such a powerful good blind-luck guesser, answer me this: how'd you know to call me Isley, instead of Tom?"

"Does it matter? Would you prefer Tom?"

"No, hell no, that ain't what I mean. Everybody calls me Isley. I ain't been called Tom in twenty years." His querulously knit brows drew in closer yet. "And by the way," he added, "while it ain't custom to ask handles in these parts, I never did cotton to being put to the social disadvantage. Makes a man feel he ain't been give his full and equal American rights. I mean, where the other feller knows who you are, but you ain't any idee who he might be. You foller me, friend?"

"You wish me to give you a name. Something you can call me. Something more tangible than friend."

"No, it don't have to be nothing more tangle-able than friend. Friend will do fine. I ain't trying to trap you."

"I know you aren't, Isley. I will tell you what. You call me Eben."

"Eben? That's an off-trail name. I never heard of it."

"It's an old Hebrew name, Isley."

"Oh? I ain't heard of them neither. Sounds like a southern tribe. Maybe Kioway or Comanche strain. Up here we got mostly Sioux and Cheyenne."

"The Hebrews weren't Indians exactly, though they were nomadic and fierce fighters. We call them Jews today."

"Oh, sure. Now, I knowed that."

"Of course you did."

They sat silent a spell, then Isley nodded.

"Well, Eben she is. Eben, what?"

"Just Eben."

"You mean like I'm just Isley?"

"Why not?"

"No good reason." Isley shrugged it off, while still bothered by it. "Well," he said, "that brings us back to where we started. How come you knowed about our trouble up here? And how come you got so far into the country without crossing trails with one side or the other? I would say this would be about the unhealthiest climate for strangers since the Grahams and Tewksburys had at it down in Arizony Territory. I don't see how you got ten miles past Casper, let alone clear up here into the Big Horn country."

Eben laughed. It was a quiet laugh, soft and friendly.

"You've provided material to keep us up all night," he said. "Let us just say that I go where trouble is, and that I know how to find my way to it."

Isley squinted at him, his own voice soft with seriousness.

"You're right; we'd best turn in. As for you and finding trouble, I got just this one say to say: I hope you're as good at sloping away from it as you are at stumbling onto it."

The other nodded thoughtfully, face sad again.

"Then, this Wolf Mountain War is as bad as I believed," he said.

"Mister," replied Isley, "when you have put your foot into this mess, you have not just stepped into *anybody's* cow chip; you have lit with both brogans square in the middle of the granddaddy pasture flapjack of them all."

"Colorful"—Eben smiled wryly—"but entirely accurate I fear. I hope I'm not too late."

"For what?" asked Isley. "It can't be stopped, for it's already started."

"I didn't mean too late to stop it, I meant too late to see justice done. That's the way I was in Pleasant Valley; too late, too late—"

He let it trail off, as Isley's eyes first widened, then narrowed, with suspicion.

"You was *there*?" he said, "in that Graham-Tewksbury feud?"

"I was there; I was not in the feud."

"Say!" said Isley enthusiastically, curiosity overcoming doubt, "who the hell won that thing, anyways; the sheepmen or the cattlemen? Naturally, we're some interested, seeing how we got the same breed of cat to skin up here."

"Neither side won," said Eben. "Neither side ever wins a war. The best that can be done is that some good comes out of the bad; that, in some small way, the rights of the innocent survive."

Isley, like most simple men of his time, had had the Bible read to him in his youth. Now he nodded again.

"You mean 'the meek shall inherit the earth'?" he asked.

"That's close," admitted his companion. "But they never inherit anything but the sins of the strong, unless they have help in time. That's what worries me. There's always so much trouble and so little time."

"That all you do, mister? Go around looking for trouble to mix into?"

"It's enough, Isley." The other smiled sadly. "Believe me it is enough."

The little cowboy shook his head.

"You know something, Eben," he said honestly. "I think you're a mite touched."

The pale youth sighed, his soft curls moving in assent.

"Do you know something, Isley?" he answered. "I have never been to any place where the men did not say the same thing. . . ."

Next morning the early snow clouds were still lying heavy to the north, but the wind had quieted. Breakfast was a lot cheerier than last night's supper, and it turned out the newcomer wasn't such a nut as Isley had figured. He wasn't looking for trouble, at all, but for a job the same as everybody else. What he really wanted was some place to hole in for the winter. He asked Isley about employment prospects at the K-Bar, and was informed they were somewhat scanter than bee tracks in a blizzard. Especially, said Isley, for a boy who looked as though he had never been caught on the blister end of a shovel.

Eben assured the little rider that he could work and Isley, more to show him to the other hands than thinking Old Man Reston would put him on, agreed to let him ride along in with him to the homeplace. Once there, though, things took an odd turn and Isley was right back to being confused about his discovery.

As far as the other hands went, they didn't make much of the stranger. They thought he looked as though he had wintered pretty hard last year, hadn't come on with the spring grass. Most figured he wouldn't make it through another cold snap. To the man, they allowed that the Old Man would eat him alive. That is, providing he showed the gall to go on up to the big house and insult the old devil's intelligence by telling him to his bare face that he aimed to hit him for work. A cow ranch in October is no place to be looking for gainful employment. The fact this daunsy stray didn't know that, stamped him a real rare tinhorn. Naturally, the whole bunch traipsed up to the house and spied through the front room window to see the murder committed. Isley got so choused up over the roostering the boys were giving his protégé that, in a moment of sheer inspiration, he offered to cover all Reston money in the crowd. He was just talking, but his pals decided to charge him for the privilege. By the time he had taken the last bet, he was in hock for his wages up to the spring roundup. And, by the time he had gotten up to the house door with Eben in tow, he would have gladly given twice over that amount to be back out on the Wolf Mountain flats or, indeed, any other place as many miles from the K-Bar owner's notoriously lively temperament.

He was stuck, though, and would not squeal. With more courage than Custer's bugler blowing the second charge at the

Little Big Horn, he raised his hand and rapped on the ranch-house door. He did bolster himself with an underbreath blasphemy, however, and Eben shook his head and said, "Take not the name of the Lord thy God in vain, Isley. Remember, your strength is as the strength of ten." Isley shot him a curdled look. Then he glanced up at the sky. "Lord, Lord," he said, "what have I done to deserve this?" He didn't get any answer from above, but did draw one from within. It suggested in sulfuric terms that they come in and close the door after them. As well, it promised corporal punishment for any corral mud or shred of critter matter stomped into the living-room rug, or any time consumed, past sixty seconds, in stating the grievance, taking no for an answer, and getting the hell back outside where they belonged.

Since the offer was delivered in the range bull's bellow generally associated with H. F. Reston, Senior, in one of his mellower states, Isley hastened to take it up.

"Mr. Reston," he said, once safe inside and the door heeled shut, "this here is Eben, and he's looking for work."

Henry Reston turned red, then white. He made a sound like a sow grizzly about to charge. Then he strangled it, waited for his teeth to loosen their clamp on one another, waved toward the door and said, "Well, he couldn't be looking for it in better company, Isley. Good luck to the both of you."

"What?" said Isley in a smothered way.

"You heard me. And don't slam the door on your way out."

"But Mr. Reston, sir—"

"Isley." The older man got up from his desk. He was the size of an agey buffalo, and had the sweetness too. "You remember damned well what I told you when you drug that last bum in here. Now you want to run a rest camp for all the drifters and sick stock that comes blowing into the barnyard with every first cold spell, you hop right on it. I'm trying to run a cow ranch, not a winter resort. Now you get that pilgrim out of here. You come back in twenty minutes, I'll have your check."

Isley was a man who would go so far. He wasn't a fighter but he didn't push too well. When he got his tail up and dropped his horns, he would stand his ground with most.

"I'll wait for it right here," he said.

"Why, you banty-legged little sparrowhawk, who the hell do you think you're telling what you'll do? *Out!*"

"*Mr. Reston—*" The stranger said it so quietly that it hit into the angry air louder than a yell. "Mr. Reston," he went on, "you're frightened. There is no call to take out your fears on Isley. Why not try me?"

"*You?*"

The Old Man just stared at him.

Isley wished he was far, far away. He felt very foolish right then. He couldn't agree more with the way the Old Man had said "you." Here was this pale-faced, skinny drifter with the downy beard, soft eyes, quiet voice and sweet smile standing there in his rags and tatters and patches and, worst of all, his farmer's runover flat boots; here he was standing there looking like something the cat would have drug in but didn't have the nerve to; and here he was standing there with all that going against him and still telling the biggest cattleman in the Big Horn basin to wind up and have a try at *him!* Well, Isley thought, in just about two seconds the Old Man was going to tie into him with a list of words that would raise a blood blister on a rawhide boot. That is, if he didn't just reach in the desk drawer, fetch out his pistol and shoot him dead on the spot.

But Isley was only beginning to be wrong.

"Well," breathed Henry Reston at last, "try you, eh?" He rumbled across the room to come to a halt in front of the slight and silent mule rider. He loomed wide as a barn door, tall as a wagon tongue. But he didn't fall in on the poor devil the way Isley had feared. He just studied him with a very curious light in his faded blue eyes and finally added, "And just what, in God's name, would you suggest I try you *at*?"

"Anything. Anything at all."

Reston nodded. "Pretty big order."

The other returned the nod. "Would a man like you take a small order?"

The owner of the K-Bar jutted his jaw. "You ain't what you let on to be," he challenged. "What do you want here?"

"What Isley told you—a job."

"What brought you here?"

"There's trouble here."

"You like trouble?"

"No."

"Maybe you're a troublemaker."

"No. I make peace when I can."

"And when you can't?"

"I still try."

"You think me giving you a winter's work is going to help you along that path?"

"Yes. Otherwise, I wouldn't be here."

Again Henry Reston studied him. Reston was not, like Tom Isley, a simple man. He was a very complicated and powerful and driving man, and a dangerous man, too.

"I make a lot of noise when I'm riled," he said to the drifter. "Don't let that fool you. I'm a thinking man."

"If you weren't," said the other, "I wouldn't be asking to work for you. I know what you are."

"But I don't know what you are, eh, is that it?"

"No, I'm just a man looking for work. I always pay my way. If there's no work for me, I travel on. I don't stay where there's no job to do."

"Well, there's no job for you here in Big Horn basin."

"You mean not that you know of."

"By God! don't try to tell me what I mean, you ragamuffin!"

"What we are afraid of, we abuse. Why do you fear me?"

Reston looked at him, startled.

"I? Fear you? You're crazy. You're not right in the head. I'm Henry F. Reston. I own this damned country!"

"I know; that's why I'm here."

"Now, what the devil do you mean by that?"

"Would the men in the valley give me work? They're poor. They haven't enough for themselves."

"How the hell do you know about the men in the valley?"

"I told you, Mr. Reston. There's trouble here. It's why I came. Now will you give me work, so that I may stay?"

"No! I'm damned if I will. Get out. The both of you!"

Isley started to sneak for the door, but Eben reached out and touched him on the arm. "Wait," he said.

"By God!" roared Reston, and started for the desk drawer. But Eben stopped him, too, as easily as he had Isley.

"Don't open the drawer," he said. "You don't need a pistol. A pistol won't help you."

Reston came around slowly. To Isley's amazement, he showed real concern. This white-faced tumbleweed had him winging.

"Won't help me what?" he asked, scowlingly.

"Decide about me."

"Oh? Well, now, you ain't told me yet what it is I've got to decide about you. Except maybe whether to kill you or have you horsewhipped or drug on a rope twice around the bunkhouse. Now you tell me what needs deciding, past that."

"I want work."

Henry Reston started to turn red again, and Isley thought he would go for the drawer after all. But he did not.

"So you want work?" he said. "And you claim you can do anything? And you got the cheek to hair up to me and say, slick and flip, 'try me.' Well, all right, By God, I'll do it. Isley—"

"Yes, sir, Mr. Reston?"

"Go put that Black Bean horse in the bronc chute. Hang the bucking rig on him and clear out the corral."

"Good Lord, Mr. Reston, that outlaw ain't been rode since he stomped Charlie Tackaberry. He's ruint three men and—"

"You want your job back, Isley, saddle him."

"But—"

"Right now."

"No, sir." Isley began, hating to face the cold with no job, but knowing he couldn't be party to feeding the mule-rider to Black Bean, "I don't reckon I need your pay, Mr. Reston. Me and Eben will make out. Come on, Ebe."

He began to back out, but Eben shook his head.

"We need the work, Isley. Go saddle the horse."

"You don't know this devil! He's a killer."

"I've faced them before, Isley. Lots of them. Saddle him."

"You, a bronc stomper? Never. I bet you ain't been on a bucker in your whole life."

"I wasn't talking about horses, Isley, but about killers."

"No, sir," insisted the little cowboy stoutly, "I ain't a'going to do it. Black Bean will chew you up fine. It ain't worth it to do it for a miserable winter's keep. Let's go."

Eben took hold of his arm. Isley felt the grip. It took him like the talons of an eagle. Eben nodded.

"*Isley,*" he said softly, "*saddle the horse.*"

The K-Bar hands got the old horse in the chute and saddled without anybody getting crippled. He had been named Black Bean from the Texas Ranger story of Bigfoot Wallace, where the Mexican general made the captive rangers draw a bean, each, from a pottery jug of mixed black and white ones; and the boys who got white beans lived and the boys who got black ones got shot. It was a good name for that old horse.

Isley didn't know what to expect of his friend by now. But he knew from long experience what to expect of Black Bean. The poor drifter would have stood a better chance going against the Mexican firing squad.

The other K-Bar boys *thought* they knew what was bound to take place. This dude very plainly had never been far enough around the teacup to find the handle. He was scarce man enough to climb over the bronc chute to get on Black Bean, let alone to stay on him long enough for them to get the blindfold off and the gate swung open.

But Isley wasn't off the pace as far as that. He knew Eben had *something* in mind. And when the thin youth had scrambled over the chute poles and more fallen, than fitted, into the bucking saddle, the other hands sensed this too. They quit roostering and hoorawing the pilgrim and got downright quiet. One or two—Gant Callahan and Deece McKayne, first off—actually tried helping at the last. Gant said, "Listen, buddy, don't try to stay with him. Just flop off the minute he gets clear of the gates. We'll scoop you up 'fore he can turn on you." Deece hung over the chute bars and whispered his advice, but Isley, holding Black Bean's head, heard him. What he said was, "See that top bar crost the gateposts? Reach for it the minute Isley whips off the blind. Hoss will go right on out from under you, and all you got to do is skin on up over the pole and set tight. You'll get spurred some by the boys, but I don't want to be buryin' you in a feedsack, you hear?"

Fact was that, between Gant and Deece giving him last-minute prayers and the other boys getting quiet, the whole operation slowed down to where the Old Man yelled at Isley to pull the blind, and for Wil Henniger to jerk the gate pin, or get out of the way and leave somebody else do it—while they were on their way up to the big house to pick up their pay. Being October and with that early blizzard threatening, he had them where the hair was short. Wil yelled out, "Powder River, let 'er buck!" and flung wide the gate. Isley pulled the blind and jumped for his life.

Well, what followed was the biggest quiet since Giggles La Chance decided to show up for church on Easter Sunday. And seeings that Giggles hadn't heard a preacher, wore a hat, or been seen abroad in daylight for six years, that was some quiet.

What Black Bean did, sure enough deserved the tribute, however. And every bit as much as Giggles La Chance.

Moreover, there was a connection between the two; the Devil seemed involved, somehow, with both decisions.

That old horse, which had stomped more good riders into the corral droppings than any sun-fisher since the Strawberry Roan, came out of that bucking chute on a sidesaddle trot, mincy and simpery as an old maid bell mare. He went around the corral bowing his neck and blowing out through his nostrils and rolling back those wally-mean eyes of his soft and dewy as a cow elk with a new calf. He made the circuit once around and brought up in front of the chute gate and stopped and spread out and stood like a five-gaited Kentucky saddlebred on the show stand; and that big quiet got so deep-still that when Dutch Hafner let out his held wind and said, *"Great Gawd Amighty!"* you'd have thought he'd shot off a cannon in a cemetery four o'clock of Good Friday morning.

Isley jumped and said, "Here, don't beller in a man's ear trumpet thataway!" and then got down off the chute fence and wandered off across the ranch lot talking to himself.

The others weren't much better off, but it was Old Man Reston who took it hardest of all.

That horse had meant a lot to him. He'd always sort of looked up to him. He was a great deal the same temperament as Old Henry. Mean and tough and smart and fearing neither God nor Devil nor any likeness of either which walked on two legs.

Now, there he was out there making moony-eyes at the seedy drifter, and damn fools out of Henry F. Reston and the whole K-Bar crew.

It never occurred to Old Henry, as it later did to Isley, that Eben had done about the same thing to him, Reston, in his living room up to the ranch house, as he'd done to Black Bean in the bucking chute: which was to buffalo him out of a full gallop right down to a dead walk, without raising either voice or hand to do it. But by the time Isley got this figured out, there wasn't much of a way to use the information. Old Henry, cast down by losing his outlaw horse and made powerful uneasy by the whole performance, had given Isley his pay, and Eben fifteen dollars for his ride—the normal fee for bronc breaking in those parts—and asked them both to be off the K-Bar by sunset. Eben had offered the fifteen dollars to the Old Man for Black Bean, when he had heard him order Deece and Gant to take the old horse out and shoot him for wolf bait. Old Henry had allowed it was a Pecos swap to take anything for such a shambles, by which he meant an outright steal. But he was always closer with a dollar than the satin over a Can-Can dancer's seat, and so he took the deal, throwing in the bucking saddle, a good split-ear bridle and a week's grub in a greasy sack, to boot. It was maybe an hour short of sundown when Isley, riding Eben's mule, and Eben astride the denatured killer, Black Bean, came to the west line of the K-Bar, in company with their escort.

"Well," said Dutch Hafner, "yonder's Bull Pine. Good luck, but don't come back."

Isley looked down into the basin of the Big Horn, sweeping from the foot of the ridge upon which they sat their horses, as far as the eye might reach, westward to Cody, Pitchfork, Meeteetse and the backing sawteeth of the Absoroka Range. The little puncher shook his head, sad, like any man, to be leaving home at only age forty-four.

"I dunno, Dutch," he mourned, "what's to become of us? There ain't no work in Bull Pine. Not for a cowhand. Not, especially, for a K-Bar cowhand."

"That's the gospel, Isley," said Deece McKayne, helpfully. "Fact is, was I you, I wouldn't scarce dast go inter Bull Pine, let alone inquire after work."

Gant Callahan, the third member of the honor guard, nodded his full agreement. "You cain't argue them marbles, Isley. Bull Pine ain't hardly nothing but one big sheep camp. I wisht there was something I could add to what Dutch has said, but there ain't. So good luck, and ride wide around them woollies."

Isley nodded back in misery. "My craw's so shrunk it wouldn't chamber a piece of pea gravel," he said. "I feel yellow as mustard without the bite."

"Yellow, hell!" snapped big Dutch, glaring at Deece and Gant. "These two idjuts ain't to be took serious, Isley. Somebody poured their brains in with a teaspoon, and got his arm joggled at that. Ain't no sheepman going to go at a cowboy in broad day, and you'll find work over yonder in the Pitchfork country. Lots of ranches there."

"Sure," said Isley, "and every one of them on the sharp lookout for a broke-down line rider and a pale-face mule wrangler to put on for the winter. Well, anyways, so long."

The three K-Bar hands raised their gloves in a mutually waved, "So long, Isley," and turned their horses back for the snug homeplace bunkhouse. Isley pushed up the collar of his worn blanket coat. The wind was beginning to spit a little sleet out of the north. It was hardly an hour's ride down the ridge and out over the flat to Bull Pine. Barring that, the next settlement—in cow country—was Greybull, on the river. That would take them till midnight to reach, and if this sleet turned to snow and came on thick—well, the hell with that, they had no choice. A K-Bar cowboy's chances in a blue norther were better than he could expect in a small-flock sheeptown like Bull Pine. Shivering, he turned to Eben.

"Come on," he said, "we got a six-hour ride."

The gentle drifter held back, shading his eyes and peering out across the basin. "Strange," he said, "it doesn't appear to be that far."

"Whoa up!" said Isley, suddenly alarmed. "What don't appear to be that far?"

"Why, Bull Pine, of course," replied the other, with his sad-soft smile. "Where else would we go?"

Isley could think of several places, one of them a sight warmer than the scraggly ridge they were sitting on. But he didn't want to be mean or small with the helpless pilgrim, no matter he had gotten him sacked and ordered off the K-Bar for good. So he didn't mention any of the options, but only shivered again and made a wry face and said edgily:

"I'd ought to know better than to ask, Ebe; but, why for we want to go to Bull Pine?"

"Because," said the bearded wanderer, "that's where the trouble is."

Eben was right. Bull Pine was where the trouble was.

All the past summer and preceding spring the cattlemen had harassed the flocks of the sheepmen in the lush pastures of the high country around the basin. Parts of flocks and whole flocks had been stampeded and run to death. Some had been put over cliffs. Some cascaded into the creeks. Others just plain chased till their hearts stopped. Nor had it been all sheep. A Basque herder had died and five Valley men had been hurt defending their flocks. So far no cattleman had died, nor even been hit, for it was they who always made the first jump and mostly at night. Now the sheepmen had had all they meant to take.

Those high country pastures were ninety percent government land, and the sheep had just as much right to them as the cattle. More right, really, because they were better suited to use by sheep than cattle. But the country, once so open and free and plenty for all, was filling up. Even in the twenty years since Isley was young, the Big Horn basin had grown six new towns and God alone knew how many upcreek, shoestring cattle ranches. The sheep had come in late, though, only about ten years back. Bull Pine was the first, and sole, sheeptown in northwest Wyoming, and it wasn't yet five years old. The cattlemen, headed by Old Henry Reston, meant to see that it didn't get another five years older, too. And Isley knew what Eben couldn't possibly know: that the early blizzard, threatening now by the hour, was all the cattlemen had been waiting for. Behind its cover they meant to sweep down on Bull Pine in a fierce raid of the haying pens and winter sheds along the river. These shelters had been built in a community effort of the valley sheep ranchers working together to accomplish what no two

or three or ten of them could do working alone. They were a
livestockmen's curiosity known about as far away as Colorado,
Utah and Montana. They had proved unbelievably successful
and if allowed to continue uncontested, it might just be that the
concept of winter feeding sheep in that country would catch on.
If it did, half the honest cattlemen in Wyoming could be out of
business. On the opposite hand, if some natural disaster should
strike the Bull Pine feedlots—say like the fences giving way in a
bad snowstorm—why then the idea of winter-feeding sheep in
the valley would suffer a setback like nothing since old Brig-
ham Young's seagulls had sailed into those Mormon crickets
down by Deseret.

Knowing what he knew of the cattlemen's plan to aid nature
in this matter of blowing over the sheepmen's fences during the
first hard blizzard, Isley followed Eben into Bull Pine with all
ten fingers and his main toes crossed.

By good luck they took a wrong turn or two of the trail on the
way down off the ridge. Well, it wasn't exactly luck, either. Isley had something to do with it. But, no matter, when they
came into Bull Pine it was so dark a man needed both hands to
find his nose. Isley was more than content to have it so. Also,
he would have been well pleased to have been allowed to stay
out in front of the General Store holding the mounts, while
Eben went within to seek the loan of some kind soul's shearing
shed to get in out of the wind and snow for the night. But Eben
said, no, that what he had in mind would require Isley's presence. The latter would simply have to gird up his courage and
come along.

Groaning, the little K-Bar puncher got down. From the number of horses standing humpback to the wind at the hitch rail,
half the sheepmen in the basin must be inside. That they would
be so, rather than home getting set to hay their sheep through
the coming storm, worried Isley a great deal. Could it be that
the Bull Piners had some warning of the cattlemen's advance?
Was this a council of range war they were stepping into the
middle of? Isley shivered.

"Ebe," he pleaded, "please leave me stay out here and keep
our stock company. Me and them sheepmen ain't nothing in
common saving for two legs and one head and maybe so a kind

word for motherhood. Now, be a good feller and rustle on in there by your ownself and line us up a woodshed or sheep pen or hayrick to hole up in for the night.''

Eben shook his head. "No," he insisted, "you must come in with me. You are essential to the entire situation."

Isley shivered again, but stood resolute. "Listen, Ebe," he warned, "this here blizzard is a'going to swarm down the valley like Grant through Cumberland Gap. We don't get under cover we're going to be froze as the back of a bronze statue's lap. Or like them poor sheep when Old Henry and his boys busts them loose in the dark of dawn tomorry."

"It's Old Henry and the others I'm thinking of," said Eben quietly. "We must be ready for them. Come along."

But Isley cowered back. "Ebe," he said, "I know that kicking never done nobody but a mule no good. Still, I got to plead self-defense, here. So don't crowd me. I'm all rared back, and I ain't a'going in there conscious."

He actually drew up one wrinkled boot as though he would take a swing at the drifter. But Eben only smiled and, for the second time, put his thin hand on Isley's arm. Isley felt the power of those slender fingers. They closed on his arm, and his will, like a Number 6 lynx trap.

"Come on, Isley," said the soft voice, "I need your testimony." And Isley groaned once more and put his head down into his collar as deep as it would go, and followed his ragged guide into the Bull Pine General Store.

"Friends," announced Eben, holding up his hands as the startled sheepmen looked up at him from their places around the possum-belly stove, "Brother Isley and I have come from afar to help you in your hour of need; please hear us out."

"That bent-legged little stray," dissented one member immediately, "never come from no place to help no sheepman. I smell cowboy! Fetch a rope, men."

Eben gestured hurriedly, but it did no good. A second valley man growled, "Ain't that Tom Isley as works for Henry Reston?" And a third gnarled herder rasped, "You bet it is! Never mind the rope, boys; I'll knock his head open, barehanded."

The group surged forward, the hairy giant who had spoken last in the lead. Eben said no more, but did not let them beyond him to the white-faced K-Bar cowboy.

As the burly leader drew abreast of him, the drifter reached out and took him gently by one shoulder. He turned him around, got a hip into his side, threw him hard and far across the floor and up against the dry-goods counter, fifteen feet away. The frame building shook to its top scantling when the big man landed. He knocked a three-foot hole in the floor, ending up hip-deep in a splintered wedging of boards from which it took the combined efforts of three friends and the storekeeper's two-hundred-pound daughter to extract him.

By the time he was freed and being revived by a stimulant-restorative composed of equal parts of sheep-dip and spirits of camphorated oil, the rest of the assemblage was commencing to appreciate the length and strength of the drifter's throw. And, realizing these things, they were politely moving back to provide him the room he had requested in the first place. Eben made his address direct and nippy.

They had come down out of the hills, he said, bearing news of invading Philistines. They were not there to become a part of the Wolf Mountain War, but to serve in what small way they might, to bring that unpleasantness to a peaceful conclusion, with freedom and justice for all. Toward that end, he concluded, his bowlegged friend had something to say that would convince the sheep raisers that he came to them, not as a kine herder bearing false prophecies, but as a man of their own simple cloth, who wanted to help them as were too honest and God-fearing to help themselves at the cattlemen's price of killing and maiming their fellow men by gunfire and in the dead of night when decent men were sleeping and their flocks on peaceful, unguarded graze.

This introduction served to interest the Bull Pine men and terrify Tom Isley. He was not up on kine herders, Philistines and false prophets, but he knew sheepmen pretty well. He reckoned he had maybe thirty seconds to fill the flush Eben had dealt him, before somebody thought of that rope again. Glancing over, he saw Big Sam Yawkey—the fallen leader of the meeting—beginning to snort and breathe heavy from the sheep-dip fumes. Figuring Big Sam to be bright-eyed and bushy-tailed again in about ten of those thirty seconds, it cut things really fine.

Especially, when he didn't have the least, last notion what the heck topic it was that Eben expected him to take off on. "Ebe!" he got out in a strangulated whisper, "what in the name of Gawd you expect me to talk about?" But the Good Samaritan with the moth-eaten mule and the one thin army blanket wasn't worried a whit. He just put out his bony hand, touched his small companion on the shoulder and said, with his soft smile, as the sheepmen closed in:

"Never fear, Isley; you will think of something."

And, for a fact, Isley did.

"Hold off!" he yelled, backing to the hardware counter and picking himself a pick handle out of a barrel of assorted tool hafts. "I'll lay you out like Samson with that jackass jaw-bone!"

The sheepmen coagulated, came to a halt.

"Now, see here," Isley launched out, "Ebe's right. I'm down here to do what I can to settle this fight. There's been far too much blood spilt a'ready. And I got an idee, like Ebe says, how to stop this here war quicker'n you can spit and holler howdy. But it ain't going to be risk-free. Monkeying around with them cattlemen is about as safe as kicking a loaded pole-cat. They're touchier than a teased snake, as I will allow you all know."

Several of the sheepmen nodded, and one said; "Yes, we know, all right. And so do you. You're one of them!"

"No!" denied Isley, "that ain't so. Mr. Reston thrun me off the K-Bar this very day. Ebe, here, made him look some small in front of the boys, and the Old Man ordered us both took to the west line and told to keep riding. I got included on account I drug Ebe in off the range, and Old Henry, he said I could keep him, seeing's I'd found him first."

His listeners scowled and looked at one another. This bow-legged little man had been punching cattle too long. He had clearly gone astray upstairs and been given his notice because of it. But they would hear him out, as none of them wanted to be flung against the dry-goods counter, or skulled with that pick handle.

"Go ahead," growled Big Sam Yawkee, coming up groggily to take his place in front of the Bull Piners. "But don't be over-long with your remarks. I done think you already stretched the blanket about as far as she will go. But, by damn, if there's a sick lamb's chance that you *do* have some way we can get back at them murderers, we ain't going to miss out on it. Fire away."

"Thank you, Mr. Yawkey," said Isley, and fired.

The idea he hit them with was as much a surprise to him as to them. He heard the words coming out of his mouth but it was as though somebody else was pulling the wires and making his lips flap. He found himself listening with equal interest to that of the Bull Pine sheepmen to his own wild-eyed plan for am-bushing the cattlemen in Red Rock Corral.

It was beautifully simple:

Red Rock Corral was a widened-out place in the middle of that squeezed-in center part of Shell Canyon called the Nar-rows. If you looked at the Narrows as a sort of rifle barrel of bedrock, then Red Rock Corral would be like a place midways of the barrel where a bullet with a weak charge had stuck, then been slammed into by the following, full-strength round, bulging the barrel at that spot. It made a fine place to catch range mustangs, for example. All you had to do was close off both ends of the Narrows, once you had them in the bulge. Then just leave them there to starve down to where they would lead out peaceful as muley cows.

Isley's idea was that what would work for tough horses would work for tough men.

The sheepmen knew for a fact, he said, that the hill trail came down to the basin through Shell Canyon. Now, if added to this, they also knew for a fact, as Isley did, that Old Henry and his boys were coming down that trail early tomorrow to knock over their winter feed pens and stampede their sheep into the bliz-zard's deep snow, why then, they would be catching up to the first part of the Isley Plan.

Pausing, the little cowboy offered them a moment to con-sider the possibilities. Big Sam was the first to recover.

"You meaning to suggest," he said, heavy voice scraping like a burro with a bad cold, "that we bottle them cattlemen up in Red Rock Corral and starve them into agreeing to leave us be? Why, I declare you're balmier than you look, cowboy. In fact, you're nervier than a busted tooth. You think we need you to tell us about ambushing? That's the cattlemen's speed. And you can't go it without people getting hurt, kilt likely. Boys," he said, turning to the others, "some deck is shy a joker, and this is him. Fetch the rope."

"No! Wait!" cried Isley, waving his pick handle feebly. "I ain't done yet."

"Oh, yes, you are," rumbled Big Sam, moving forward.

Yet, as before, he did not reach Tom Isley.

Eben raised his thin, pale hand and Big Sam brought up as short as though he had walked into an invisible wall.

"What the hell?" he muttered, rubbing his face, frightened. "I must be losing my marbles. Something just clouted me acrost the nose solid as a low limb."

"It was your conscience." Eben smiled. "Isley has more to say. Haven't you, Isley?"

The little cowboy shook his head, bewildered.

"Hell, don't ask me, Ebe; you're the ventrillyquist."

"Speak on"—his friend nodded—"and be not afraid."

"Well," said Isley, "I'll open my mouth and see what comes out. But I ain't guaranteeing nothing."

Big Sam Yawkey, still rubbing his nose, glared angrily.

"Something better come out," he promised, "or I'll guarantee you something a sight more substantial than nothing; and that's to send you out of town with your toes down. You've got me confuseder than a blind dog in a butcher shop, and I'm giving you one whole minute more to hand me the bone, or down comes your doghouse."

"Yeah!" snapped a burly herder behind him. "What you take us for, a flock of ninnies? Jest because we run sheep don't mean we got brains to match. And you suggesting that we set a wild hoss trap for them gunslingers and night riders of Old Man Reston's is next to saying we're idjuts. You think we're empty-headed enough to buy any such sow bosom as holding them cat-

tlemen in that rock hole with a broomtail brush fence on both
ends?''

"No," said Isley calmly, and to his own amazement, *"but
you might trying doing it with blasting powder."*

"What!" shouted Yawkey.

"Yes, sir," said Isley meekly, "a half can of DuPont Number 9 at each end, touched off by a signal from the bluff above.
When all of them have rode into Red Rock Corral, down comes
the canyon wall, above and below, and there they are shut off
neat as a newborn calf, and nobody even scratched. I'd say that
with this big snow that's coming, and with the thermometer
dropping like a gut-shot elk, they'd sign the deed to their baby
sister's virtue inside of forty-eight hours.''

There was silence, then, as profound as the pit.

It was broken, presently, by Big Sam's awed nod, and by
him clearing his throat shaky and overcome as though asked to
orate in favor of the flag on Independence Day.

"Great Gawd A'mighty, boys," he said, "it might work!"

And the rush for the front door and the horses standing back-
humped at the hitch rail, was on.

As a matter of Big Horn basin record, it did work.

The Bull Piners got their powder planted by three A.M., and
about four, down the trail came the deputation from the hills.
The snow was already setting in stiff, and they were riding
bunched tight. Big Sam Yawkey fired his Winchester three
times when they were all in the middle of Red Rock Corral and
Jase Threepersons, the storekeeper, and Little Ginger, his two-
hundred-pound daughter, both lit off their respective batches of
DuPont Number 9 above and below the corral so close together
the cattlemen thought it was one explosion and Judgment Day
come at last.

Well, it had, in a way.

And, as Isley had predicted, it came in less than forty-eight
hours.

The sheepmen were mighty big about it. They lowered down
ropes with all sorts of bedding and hot food and even whiskey
for the freezing ranchers, as well as some of their good baled

sheep hay for the horses. But they made it clear, through Big Sam's bellowed-down advice, that they meant to keep their friends and neighbors from the hills bottled up in that bare-rock bulge till the new grass came, if need be. They wouldn't let them starve, except slowly, or freeze, unless by accident. But they had come out from Bull Pine to get a truce, plus full indemnity for their summer's sheep losses, and they were prepared to camp up on that bluff—in the full comfort of their heated sheep wagons—from right then till Hell, or Red Rock Corral, froze over.

That did it.

There was some hollering back and forth between the two camps for most of that first day. Then it got quiet for the better part of the second. Then, along about sundown, Old Henry Reston yelled up and said: "What's the deal, Yawkey? We don't get back to our stock, right quick, we won't have beef enough left to hold a barbecue."

Big Sam read them the terms, which Isley wasn't close enough to hear. Reston accepted under profane duress and he and Big Sam shook on the matter. Naturally, such a grip had the force of law in the basin. Once Old Henry and Big Sam had put their hands to an agreement, the man on either side who broke that agreement might just as well spool his bed and never stop moving.

Realizing this, Isley modestly stayed out of the affair. There were other inducements toward laying low and keeping back from the rim while negotiations went forward and concluded. One of these was the little cowboy's certain knowledge of what his fellow K-Bar riders would think of a cowman who sold out to a bunch of sheepherders. Even more compelling was the cold thought as to what they would *do* to such a hero, should they ever catch up to the fact that he had plotted the whole shameful thing. All elements, both of charming self-effacement and outright cowardice, considered, Isley believed himself well advised to saddle up and keep traveling. This he planned to do at the first opportunity. Which would be with the night's darkness in about twenty minutes. It was in carrying out the first part of this strategy—rounding up Eben and their two mounts—that he ran into the entertainment committee from the Bull Pine camp;

three gentlemen sheepherders delegated by their side to invite Isley to the victory celebration being staged in his honor at the Ram's Horn Saloon later that evening.

Isley, confronted with this opportunity, refused to be selfish. He bashfully declined the credit being so generously offered, claiming that it rightfully belonged to another. When pressed for the identity of this hidden champion, he said that of course he meant his good friend Eben. "You know," he concluded, "the skinny feller with the white face and curly whiskers. Ebe," he called into the gathering dusk past the hay wagon where they had tied Black Bean and the mule, "come on out here and take a bow!"

But Eben did not come out, and Jase Threepersons, the chairman of the committee, said to Isley, "What skinny feller with what white face and what curly whiskers?"

He said it in a somewhat uncompromising manner and Isley retorted testily, "The one that was with me in the store; the one what thrun Big Sam acrost the floor. Damn it, what you trying to come off on me, anyhow?"

Jase looked at him and the other two sheepmen looked at him and Jase said, in the same flat way as before, "*You* thrun Big Sam agin that counter. There wasn't nobody in that store with you. What *you* trying to come off on *us,* Tom Isley?"

"Blast it!" cried Isley. "I never laid a finger on Big Sam. You think I'd be crazy enough to try that?"

The three shook their heads, looking sorrowful.

"Evidently so," said Jase Threepersons.

"No, now you all just hold up a minute," said Isley, seeing their pitying looks. "Come on, I'll show you. Right over here ahint the hay wagon. Me and Ebe was bedded here last night and boilt our noon coffee here today. I ain't seen him the past hour, or so, and he may have lost his nerve and lit out, but, by damn, I can show you where his mule was tied and I'll fetch *him* for you, give time."

They were all moving around the wagon, as he spoke, Isley in the lead. He stopped, dead. "No!" they heard him say. "My God, it cain't be!" But when they got up to him, it was. There was no sign of a double camp whatever. And no sign of the bearded stranger, nor of his moth-eaten mule. "He was right here!'' yelled Isley desperately. "Damn it, you saw him, you're just funning, just hoorawing me. You seen him and you seen that broke-down jackass he rides; who the hell you think I been talking to the past three days, *myself*?"

" 'Pears as if." Jase nodded sympathetically. "Too bad, too. Little Ginger had kind of took a shine to you. Wanted me to see you stuck around Bull Pine a spell. But, seeing the way things are with you, I reckon she'd best go back to waiting out Big Sam."

"Yes, sir, thank you very much, sir," said Isley gratefully, "but I still aim to find Ebe and that damn mule for you." He bent forward with sudden excitement. "Say, lookit here! Mule tracks leading off! See? What'd I tell you? Old Ebe, he's a shy cuss, and mightily humble. He didn't want no thanks. He'd done what he come for—stopped the trouble—and he just naturally snuck off when nobody was a'watching him. Come on! We can catch him easy on that stove-up old jack."

The three men came forward, stooped to examine the snow. There were some tracks there, all right, rapidly being filled by the fresh fall of snow coming on, but tracks all the same. They could have been mule tracks too. It was possible. But they could also have been smallish horse tracks. Like say left by Pettus Teague's blue-blood race mare. Or by that trim Sioux pony belonging to Charlie Bo-peep, the Basque half-breed. Or by Coony Simms's little bay. Or Nels Bofors's slim Kentucky-bred saddler. Or two, three others in the camp.

Straightening from its consideration of the evidence, the committee eyed Tom Isley.

"Isley," said Jase Threepersons, "I'll tell you what we'll do. All things took into account, you've been under consider-able strain. Moreover, that strain ain't apt to get any less when word gets back up into the hill that you come down here and hatched this ambush idea. We owe you a'plenty, and we ain't going to argue with you about that there feller and his mule. But them cowboys of Old Henry's might take a bit more convinc-ing. Now suppose you just don't be here when Big Sam and the others come up out of the corral with the K-Bar outfit. We'll say you was gone when we got here to the hay wagon, and that you didn't leave no address for sending on your mail. All right?"

Isley took a look at the weather.

It was turning off warmer, and this new snow wouldn't last more than enough to cover his tracks just nice. The wind was down, the sun twenty minutes gone and, from the rim of the bluff above the corral, sounds were floating which indicated the roping parties were pulling up the first of the K-Bar sheep raiders. To Isley, it looked like a fine night for far riding. And sudden.

He pulled his coat collar up, his hat brim down, and said to Jase Threepersons, "All right."

"We'll hold the boys at the rim to give you what start we can," said Jase. And Isley stared at him and answered, "No, don't bother; you've did more than enough for me a'ready. Good-bye, boys, and if I ever find any old ladies or dogs that need kicking, I will send them along to you."

Being sheepherders, they didn't take offense, but set off to stall the rescue party at the rim, true to their word.

Isley didn't linger to argue the morals of it. He got his blanket out from under the hay wagon, rolled it fast, hurried to tie it on behind old Black Bean's saddle. By this time he wasn't even sure who *he* was, but didn't care to take any chances on it. He just might turn out to be Tom Isley, and then it would be close work trying to explain to Dutch and Gant and Deece and the rest what it was he was doing bedded down in the sheep camp.

He had the old black outlaw swung around and headed in the same direction as the fading mule tracks—or whatever they were—in something less than five minutes flat. The going was all downhill to the river, and he made good time. About eight o'clock he came to the Willow Creek Crossing of the Big Horn, meaning to strike the Pitchfork Trail there. He was hungry and cold and the old black needed a rest, so he began to look around for a good place to lie up for the night. Imagine his surprise and pleasure, then, to spy ahead, the winky gleam and glow of a campfire, set in a snug thicket of small timber off to the right of the crossing. Following its cheery guide, he broke through the screening bush and was greeted by a sight that had him bucked up quicker than a hatful of hot coffee.

"Ebe!" he cried delightedly. "I knowed you wouldn't run out on me! God bless it, I am that pleased to see you!"

"And I likewise, Isley." The gentle-voiced drifter smiled. "Alight and thrice welcome to my lowly board."

Well, he had a wind-tight place there. It was nearly as warm and shut in from the cold as the old rock house out on Wolf Mountain flat, and he had added to it with a neat lean-to of ax-cut branches, as pretty as anything Isley had ever seen done on the range. And the smell of the rack of lamb he had broiling over the flames of his fire was enough to bring tears to the eyes of a Kansas City cow buyer.

Isley could see no legitimate reason for declining the invitation.

Falling off Black Bean, he said, "You be a'saying grace, Ebe, whilst I'm a'pulling this hull; I don't want to hold you up none when we set down—"

While they ate, things were somewhat quiet. It was very much the same as it had been when Eben came in cold and hungry to Isley's fire out on the flats. Afterward, though, with the blackened coffeepot going the rounds, Isley rolling his rice-paper smokes and Eben playing some of the lonesomest pretty tunes on his old mouth harp that the little cowboy had ever heard, the talk started flowing at a better rate.

There were several things Isley wanted to know, chief among them being the matter of the Bull Pine men letting on as if he had jumped his head hobbles. But he kept silent on this point, at first, leading off with some roundabout inquiries which wouldn't tip his hand to Eben. These were such things as how come he didn't recognize any of the tunes Eben was playing on the harp? Or how did Eben manage to evaporate from the sheep camp at Red Rock Corral without any of the Bull Piners seeing him? Or why didn't he let Isley know he was going? And how come him, Eben, to have lamb on the fire in October, when there wasn't any lamb?

To this tumble of questions, Eben only replied with his soft laugh and such put-offers as that the tunes were sheepherder songs from another land, that the fresh snowfall had hidden his departure from the hay wagon bed spot, that he knew the Bull Piners planned a party for Isley and didn't wish to stand in his way of enjoying the tribute due him, and that for him, Eben, lamb was always in season and he could put his hand to some just about as he pleased.

Well, Isley was a little mystified by this sort of round-the-barn business. But when Eben made the remark about the Bull Pine party being due him, Isley, he quit slanting his own talk, off-trail, and brought it right to the bait.

"Ebe," he said, "I'm going to ask you one question. And you mighten as well answer it, for I'm going to hang on to it like an Indian to a whiskey jug."

"Gently, gently," said the other, smiling. "You'll have your answer, but not tonight. In the morning, Isley, I promise you."

"Promise me what?" demanded the little cowboy. "I ain't even said what I wanted."

"But I know what you want, and you shall have it—in the morning."

Isley eyed him stubbornly.

"I'll have what in the morning?" he insisted.

Eben smiled that unsettling sad-sweet smile, and shrugged. *"Proof that I was with you all the while,"* he said.

Isley frowned, then nodded.

"All right, Ebe, you want to save her for sunup, that's fine with me. I'm a little wore down myself."

"You rest, then," said the drifter. "Lie back upon your saddle and your blanket, and I will read to you from a book I have." He reached in his own blanket, still curiously unrolled, and brought forth two volumes: one a regular-sized black leather Bible, the other a smallish red morocco-bound tome with some sort of outlandish foreign scripting on the cover. "The Book of the Gospel," he said, holding up the Bible; then, gesturing with the little red book, "the *Rubáiyát* of Omar Khayyám: which will you have, Isley?"

"Well," said the latter, "I can tell by some of your talk, Ebe, that you favor the Good Book, and I ain't denying that it's got some rattling-tall yarns in it. But if it's all the same to you, I'll have a shot of the other. I'm a man likes to see both sides of the billiard ball."

Eben nodded soberly, but without any hint of reproval.

"You have made your choice, Isley," he said, "and so be it. Listen . . ."

He opened the small volume then and began to read selected lines for his raptly attentive companion. Lazing back on his blanket, head propped on his saddle, the warmth of the fire reflecting in under the lean-to warm and fragrant as fresh bread, Isley listened to the great rhymes of the ancient Persian:

". . . And as the Cock crew, those who stood before
The Tavern shouted—'Open then the Door!
   'You know how little while we have to stay
   'And once departed, may return no more! . . .' "

". . . Come, fill the Cup, and in the fire of Spring
Your winter-garment of Repentance fling:
   The Bird of Time has but a little way
   To flutter—and the Bird is on the Wing. . . ."

". . . A Book of Verses underneath the Bough,
A Jug of Wine, a Loaf of Bread—and Thou
   Beside me singing in the Wilderness—
   Oh, Wilderness were Paradise enow! . . ."

". . . Yesterday this Day's Madness did prepare,
Tomorrow's Silence, Triumph, or Despair:
   Drink! for you know not whence you came, nor why:
   Drink! for you know not why you go, nor where. . . ."

". . . The Moving Finger writes; and, having writ,
Moves on: nor all your Piety nor Wit
   Shall lure it back to cancel half a Line,
   Nor all your Tears wash out a Word of it. . . ."

The poetry was done, then, and Eben was putting down the little red book to answer some drowsy questions from Isley as to the nature of the man who could write such wondrously true things about life as she is actually lived, just on a piece of ordinary paper and in such a shriveled little old leather book.

Eben reached over and adjusted Isley's blanket more

about the dozing cowboy, then told him the story of Omar Khayyám. But Isley was tired, and his thoughts dimming. He remembered, later, some few shreds of the main idea; such as that Old Omar was a tentmaker by trade, that he didn't set much store by hard work, that he didn't know beans about horses, sheep or cattle, but he was a heller on women and grape juice. Past that, he faded out and slept gentle as a dead calf. The sun was an hour high and shining square in his eye when he woke up.

He lay still a minute, not recalling where he was. Then it came to him and he sat up with a grin and a stretch and a *"Morning, Ebe,"* that was warm and cheerful enough to light a candle from. But Eben didn't answer to it. And never would. For, when Tom Isley blinked to get the climbing sun out of his eyes and took a second frowning look around the little camp-site, all he saw was the unbroken stretch of the new snow which had fallen quiet as angel's wings during the night. There was no Eben, no mule, no threadbare army blanket bedroll. And, this time, there were not even any half-filled hoofprints leading away into the snow. This time there was only the snow. And the stillness. And the glistening beauty of the new day.

Oh, and there was one other small thing that neither Tom Isley, nor anybody else in the Big Horn basin, was ever able to explain. It was a little red morocco book about four-by-six inches in size, which Isley found in his blanket when he went to spool it for riding on. Nobody in Northwest Wyoming had ever heard of it, including Tom Isley.

It was called the *Rubáiyát* of Omar Khayyám.